WELCOME TO ELSEWHERE

Anthology of Award-winning Short Stories

ISBN-13: 978-0-9742652-9-2
ISBN-10: 0-9742652-9-2

DEDICATION

This anthology is dedicated to those who visit Elsewhere daily

To the authors featured in this book: Scribes Valley thanks you for your time, patience, trust, and talent.

CONTENTS

ARRIVAL
A Foreword by David L. Repsher, editor

Greetings from the Elsewhere Welcoming Committee. We're glad you made the journey and hope your stay here is exactly what you want it to be.

Please feel free to roam wherever you want and take as long as you want. We have no timetables, no agendas, no schedules, no calendars, and no clocks. Time does not matter here. Matter of fact, nothing really matters here. Normal rules do not apply. Restrictions are non-existent. No boundaries, no "Keep Out" signs. And laws? *What* laws?

Basically, you are by yourself. You are your own tour guide in a universe of anything. So, be sure to allow yourself to see everything, read everything, and visit everywhere.

Before we turn you loose, please check any excess baggage—along with any extra close-mindedness you may have—at the door. You won't need them. Nothing is 'usual' here so you're arriving with a clean slate.

You may now proceed through the door, please watch your step, and into Elsewhere. Thanks again for coming and we'll see you again...whenever.

FIRST PLACE

HANDS OF TIME
©2010 by John Robbins

The cold air bit at my face as soon as I opened the front door. Despite the winds being southerly, the weather was still frigid, and the old pecan tree creaked and rattled its bare limbs as the wind passed through. I looked up past the burgeoning sun on the horizon to find high, wispy clouds streaked across the sky, thinking aloud, "It must be pretty windy up there too." The clouds reminded me of wind-driven snow blowing across a barren road, shifting and changing by some unseen force. I shivered as I walked over the crunchy grass toward my truck, but I sensed that conditions would be changing, knowing that the coldness I felt couldn't last much longer.

When I was younger, winter seemed to last an eternity...and colder too. Our old car stayed cold and was not much to look at, but it got us where we needed to go. When waiting for the school bus in the old car on an early winter morning, I'd put my hands on the window, melting the shape of my hand into the frost that covered the outside. The cold would slowly seep through my skin, making its way to the bone. When I couldn't take the cold any longer, I warmed up my hand between my legs. The hand-me-down corduroys made excellent hand warmers, much better than my worn-out brown jersey gloves that I was too embarrassed to wear. They were full of holes from carrying firewood and from my other chores. Once the pain faded, I'd return my hand to the exact same position to finish melting away the stubborn frost.

Steam, rushing from my nostrils in narrow white columns and disappearing into the dry winter air, brought me back to this morning's cold reality as I sighed heavily at the sight of the truck's windows. An obstinate coating of frost blanketed the windows that weren't facing the south wind, and, unfortunately, that included the windshield. The pure whiteness of the frost starkly contrasted the faded brown paint on my old Dodge. It wasn't shiny or fancy, but it got me to and from. A new truck would be nice, and I could afford it...but this one served the purpose just fine. Besides, there was something about this truck...a fond link to my past, perhaps.

The door's hinges creaked and groaned from the cold as I opened it to retrieve the ice scraper. Nothing can escape the bitterness of winter. I went ahead and started the truck and forced a smile as steam rushed from the exhaust pipes just as it did from my nose. It would take ten or fifteen minutes for warm air to blow, but once it did, the heater would practically run a person out if not turned down. I slid the soft leather glove from my hand and into my pocket and began clearing the glass. Redness and pain soon set into my fingers as the frost leapt from the glass with each pass of the scraper. I couldn't wait to put the glove back on.

Soon I rumbled on my way to work down the country road that led into Shreveport. The sun laid low on the southeastern horizon, reluctant to move fully into view. Long shadows stretched across the road like nature's sundials, marking the beginning of a new day. Turning onto the southbound highway, I grabbed my sunglasses from the dash to try and ease my squinting. For months, construction on the road turned the fairly scenic drive into a landscape of dirt and downed trees, which lay lifeless in mangled piles. The widened road would be nice once finished, but until then, I'd have to get used to the depressing view. Winter didn't help. The cold and snowless weather added to the misery.

As I topped a small rise in the road, a figure came into view on the other side. His walk was slow but determined, and he appeared to be under-dressed for the elements. As I neared him, he made no attempt to signal me for a ride, instead his gaze remained down on the road ahead. Knowing he had to be cold, I pulled over just ahead of him and waited for him to come alongside. I normally don't stop to offer rides to strangers, but something inside told me to stop for this man. Rolling down my window just far enough to converse, I asked him if he needed a ride. His gaze lifted to me. His eyes were blue and cold like the winter sky, and his face weathered like the landscape through which he walked. He nodded in acceptance and rounded my truck for the passenger door.

At first, I thought it was the winter air that came in with him, but even after the door was closed, I felt a coldness emanating from the stranger. It seemed to flow from him like frosty air spilling from an open freezer door. His gaze remained down much as it did when he was walking. His hands lay folded in his lap, not so much as if trying to warm them but rather to conceal them from view. After a moment I asked him where he needed to go.

"Downtown...riverfront...construction site...if you're headed that way," his crackly voice struggled out. His voice even sounded frozen, but each word he uttered seemed to chip away the iciness.

"No problem," I said, "That's basically on my way." It wasn't really, but it wasn't far off my route. The downtown area was small, and I knew what site he spoke of.

He began slowly rubbing his hands together, rolling one over the other, and they sounded like a cardboard box sliding across a cement floor. I stared ahead at the road, trying to think of something to say to help break the silence. My stare drifted down to the dash where the soft leather gloves lay.

"That wind will sure cut through a feller," was all I could come up with. I reverted back to how I used to talk and how I still talk when I'm around my family...I'm not sure why. Time had stripped the Arkansas hills from my voice, but I think it was something in the man's voice, a familiarity that brought it out now.

"You get used to it," he returned.

"You been walking very far?" I asked.

"Not too far, couple days off and on maybe," he said, sounding as if he truly believed his own words.

I had a hard time with it. "If ya don't mind me askin', where'd ya start off from?"

"Up near Stuttgart," was his reply as his gaze began to slowly lift from his feet.

Stuttgart, it wasn't real close to where I was raised, but close enough to branch off from the small talk. It was across the other side of the state from where I come from, mostly flatland as opposed to the hills I called home. Two days. He hadn't gotten too many rides to have only made it this far.

"Pretty good farmin' over there," I continued.

"Not this time a year," his words came faster and clearer, but sad still the same. The emptiness of the statement flooded my mind with visions of frozen earth and dry brown plants broken over from fall's harvest.

I started putting facts from our conversation together... winter, poorly clothed, hands like aged leather, walking to construction site for days, from poor farming area. I decided not to pursue my conclusion any farther. He was obviously on a desperate path, one that does not need to be pointed out with careless questions.

The silence again became overwhelming, and my stare returned to the dash, then sideways from the corner of my vision to the man's hands still clasped. I reached for the gloves and placed them between us on the seat.

"Here's an extra pair of gloves if you're interested. I got no need for 'em." That wasn't true at all.

He studied the gloves without touching them, then looked from the gloves to me and back again, and then picked them up and studied them some more. His apparent appreciation of the gloves said all that needed to be said. He slid them on, flexing his fingers like they were bending for the first time in a long time. His sad, rugged face didn't reveal it, but a smile grew in his eyes. I'm not sure if it was the heater, but the inside of my truck suddenly seemed warmer...and the ensuing silence wasn't so bad. Again I stared ahead, my thoughts wandering.

The cab of our old log truck was about as warm as the family car. The '56 International didn't have a luxurious interior, just a lot of bare metal and an uninviting vinyl seat. We hauled a lot of wood on that old truck. The whole family wouldn't have fit inside, but nonetheless, it managed to get us to a better place. Despite the layers of shirts and pants, the biting air found its way past metal, vinyl and the layers. Even the plastic bread bags I wore over my socks couldn't stop it. The bags always seemed to find their way down to my toes anyway, inching like a worm down a limb. Fortunately, cutting timber and firewood drove away the chill, and the work managed to keep our family going. We did what we had to in order to survive the dead months, and I couldn't imagine a more difficult means of doing so. The small amount of sap still left in the various trees we cut stained my hands, especially where the calluses were thickest. Each winter, the stains started out reddish-brown but turned black with time. Most kids at school were polite enough not to ask about the stains, but it didn't keep them from staring. At times I wished I had my jerseys to cover them up.

I hadn't worked like that in years, though. If they could see my hands now, I thought as my stare moved to my hands gripping the steering wheel.

Before long, we had entered the downtown area. The sun climbed higher and loosened dawn's icy grip. Looking right as I made a turn, I noticed that the same grip had eased its hold on the man. He sat more upright and was looking out the window. He raised his newly gloved hand and pointed over to the construction site.

"That's it," he said. The remark rang with optimism.

There wasn't anyone else at the site yet, so I pulled into the dirt lot and parked next to the chain fence. I turned to the man and extended my hand. He removed his glove and shook my hand. I was surprised by the strength and warmth of the exchange. His face appeared less weathered and it bore a thin smile. The eyes, once like the winter sky, were brighter and complimented the smile. He gave a nod that said everything and turned, opened the door and stepped out into the morning sun.

I pulled out of the lot back onto the street and watched him in my rearview mirror. He didn't look back at me or wave or anything...he didn't need to. He just stood there looking up at the sky with the south wind blowing in his face, and I wondered if he sensed the same change I did.

I continued my trip to work. It had become unbearably warm in the cab, so I decided to turn down the heater. Reaching for the fan switch, I realized it was already on low. I looked up to find my reflection in the rearview mirror. I wore a thin smile, too, but not a prideful smile...a grateful one that appeared as I pondered the time spent with the stranger. Time, life, and the roads we both traveled appeared as the face of a clock. The center marked common ground, and the hands marked our lives, traveling at different speeds toward some destination in time. And just as a real clock, the hands briefly met and then parted. The traffic light ahead turned yellow, bringing my thoughts back to my place in time. Turning at the light led me to work.

The parking lot alongside the building still lay in the shadows. After parking, I got out and stood silently between my truck and the car next to it. Obviously, the car had been there all night because the windows were still covered with frost. The frost was hard and white, much the same as the layer that formed on my windows overnight. I extended my soft, warm palm, fingers spread, and pressed it firmly on the window. After a moment, I pulled it away, and it didn't even feel all that cold. The melted imprint returned a smile to my face. I turned my hand over to look at the palm, and I could feel my heart surging a reviving warmth down to my fingertips. I curled and flexed them slowly, like they were bending for the first time in a long time.

About the author:

John Robbins is a meteorologist in the U.S. Air Force. He has served over 19 years on active duty and is currently stationed at Langley AFB, VA as the Superintendent of Weather Operations. John is a graduate of the Community College of the Air Force and the University of Maryland University College. John is married to Daniela Miron Robbins and has two children, Emily 13 and Andrew 10. Aside from writing and spending time with his family, John enjoys running, biking, cooking, woodworking, and volunteering.

John grew up in rural northwest Arkansas and draws inspiration from his spartan upbringing and life experiences. His goal is to continue writing stories that capture memorable snapshots of his life and share them with his children and future grandchildren.

SECOND PLACE

SNOW WOMAN
©2010 by Ronna L. Edelstein

The cabbie, forgetting to give her change or wish her a happy New Year, roars away from the curb, leaving Vera standing alone with her two suitcases, one on either side of her. The angry December wind from the nearby lake slaps her face and knocks the lighter of the two suitcases to the sidewalk. Ken and Barbie mannequins, looking red carpet perfect in tuxedo and gown, smile their plastic smiles from their window perch in *Putting on the Ritz: Formal Clothes for an Informal Price*, the store that rents the entire first floor of Vera's less-than-ritzy apartment building. At the stroke of midnight, a new year will begin, but nothing will change for twenty-three-year-old Vera. She will still share her efficiency with bags of student papers waiting to be read, will still try to teach ninth graders an appreciation of literature when they only want to be shopping or doing heaven-knows-what with heaven-knows-whom, and will still be on the outside looking through the glass at all the Kens and Barbies enjoying life.

Vera nods to the mannequins, heaves her suitcases, and stuffs her key into the foyer lock. She wonders whether she should get her mail later, but the thought of climbing, descending, and then re-climbing those two flights of stairs pushes her towards her tarnished mailbox.

Crowded between her after-Christmas catalogues and a week's worth of bills and junk mail, sits a letter in a business-sized envelope. The return address, printed in blue ink, confuses Vera. "Why would Ma write when I just got back from visiting?" Vera tosses the mail into her traveling purse, grabs her suitcases, and pants up the two flights to her cell-like efficiency. With each step she wonders what sin she inadvertently committed during her visit home that caused Ma to write.

Dad, not Ma, is the family letter writer. Vera has at least four "warm fuzzy" files of his notes, cards, and more lengthy correspondences. Ma, however, never embraced writing letters, not even in her more leisurely days before she began working at an exclusive women's clothing shop and sold her soul to the company store. Ma has always preferred the verbal approach, not wanting to squander money on a stamp or card. As the child at overnight camp and as the adult at graduate school, Vera knew not to expect mail from Ma. Vera, now the independent single woman and professional teacher, wavers between opening the epistle and burning it.

Curiosity triumphs over fear. After parking her suitcases next to the couch which also serves as her bed, Vera sits in her favorite blue corduroy easy chair and studies the envelope. It looks innocuous enough, but Vera knows better. She knows the venom that can lie behind those innocent blue letters. With shaking fingers—maybe from the cold since Vera had turned off the heat before leaving and has not bothered to turn it back on yet, but most likely from nerves—Vera unseals the envelope. As usual, Ma has not wasted time with a date or a "Dear Daughter" greeting but, in typical Ma fashion, she goes right to the point:

I have never seen you look so fat.

Vera, living up to her older brother's "Miss Niagara Falls" nickname for her, starts to cry.

How could you let yourself get so fat?

Ma's words stab Vera, puncturing her already shaky sense of self-worth. Like a robot, Vera heaves her suddenly bulkier body from the chair and unpacks the clean clothes that Ma, as always, had gotten up early to wash and iron for her. She knows Ma does her laundry to save her from trekking to the Laundromat down the street, but now Vera feels violated from this act of kindness. She pictures Ma holding up her cotton briefs and stretching the elastic waist band between her two hands as if measuring the width of Vera's hips. Ma probably regrets teaching Vera to cut out the neck tags in her shirts ("Don't they make your neck itch? They do mine!") because now Ma has no definitive evidence as to what size Vera wears (the XL tag sewn to the elastic waist band of her pants gives nothing away since Vera, even when stick thin, always buys overly large pants to hide any real or fantasized belly and bum bulges).

By the time she finishes putting away her clothes and rereading the letter for the fifth time, Vera is too tired to make dinner. She removes an almost full gallon of vanilla ice cream from her freezer, takes a soup spoon from the dish rack, grabs a handful of paper towels, and squeezes into her blue chair.

It has begun to snow. As the flakes first float to the street, they look like bits and pieces of tutus from dancing fairies. Typical for the Midwest, the snow quickly intensifies, turning the feathery flakes into chunks of white chocolate. Vera fights the urge to open her window and fill her spoon with nature's treat. She fights the urge to dash down the steps, rush out into the storm, and lie in the snow until its white tears drown her. Instead, she runs her fingers around the inside of the now empty ice cream carton to make sure she has not left behind even one small vanilla bite, and then she just sits and thinks.

The trip to see her parents had followed the same pattern of every trip home. About two weeks prior to departure, Vera had gone into panic mode. Knowing Ma would scrutinize every inch of her face and body, she had tried to substitute healthy salads for her more appealing ice cream dinners, but the more anxious she became, the more ice cream, cookies, M&M's, and pizza she devoured. By the morning of the trip, Vera knew she had failed.

She was still Vera, the girl who would never live up to Ma's golden expectations, no matter how hard she tried.

Vera hugs herself and, rocking back and forth as if in prayer, chants the childhood rhyme she has never quite understood: "Sticks and stones can break your bones, but names can never hurt you." If this is true, then why does Ma's "fat" label hurt so much? Why does it blind her to any other image of herself?

The wind blows some slivers of ice against Vera's window. She imagines they are Swarovski diamonds, each one representing a Prince Charming waiting to sweep Vera to a magical land where fountains drip with vanilla ice cream and where rivers flow with chocolate sauce. Vera remembers growing up in such a fantasy in which Ma ended every dinner with a dessert of pudding and a "subsert" of cake. She never sent Vera or her older brother to bed without first serving them a dish of ice cream—vanilla sinking under the weight of the chocolate syrup.

Yet, even as she cleaned her plate and licked her spoon and even years before she understood the word "oxymoron," Vera sensed the contradiction between Ma's actions and Ma's words. Ma's hands would be scooping out more ice cream, but her eyes would be exploding with the "you can't be too thin" message. As Vera entered puberty, Ma slowly ended the dessert-subsert-ice-cream-before-bed tradition, forcing Vera to become a closet eater who indulged her sweet tooth at school by stealing her locker partner's cookies, or at a neighbor's house by always politely accepting the "Why don't you have seconds?" suggestion. Should Ma ever detect the scent of chocolate on Vera's breath or notice the markings around her waist from too tight elastic, she would convey her disapproval by a lifting of her eyebrows, a slight shaking of her head, or an almost imperceptible frown.

No matter how subtle the message, Vera always heard it, loud and clear. Desperate for Ma's approval—if not love—Vera would spend the next days or weeks barely surviving on a hardboiled egg brunch and a lean piece of chicken or salad dinner. By the time Vera entered college, she was determined to avoid the "freshman fifteen" weight gain. She spent her entire first term in a state of dehydration, depriving herself of milk, juice, and even water in an attempt to reduce bloating and body weight.

Now, even six hundred miles away, Vera can sense her mother's watchful presence. She feels Ma's gaze when she takes a piece of fruitcake at the teacher holiday party, and she hears her "tsking" when she devours a burger and hot dog, both with buns, at the end-of-the-year barbecue. Vera goes to these events knowing she should just munch carrots or at least sacrifice the buns, but so many years of starvation have weakened her defenses. Ma, however, always seems in fine form. With this letter she has upped her offense to a new level.

Vera heaves herself out of her blue chair and begins pacing. She doesn't care about disturbing the unmarried couple downstairs because of all the nights they keep her awake by blasting their stereo; anyway, with it being New Year's Eve, they are probably out partying. Vera knows that nothing she does will bother Ken and Barbie in their window cocoon. So, she paces. From the door to the window. From the window to the door. Back and forth, like a metronome or a Grandfather Clock, she marks the passing of time.

She imagines Ma at the kitchen table writing the evil letter, just like Scrooge sitting alone at his desk and counting his money. Vera sees Ma's bony, Scrooge-like fingers as they grip the blue pen, she sees Ma's serpentine tongue pushing itself through her clenched teeth and pursed lips as she searches for the perfect poisonous words. While Ma had been busily creating names to hurt her, she and Dad had probably been watching *The Waltons* in the living room. The next morning, while she and Dad had most likely gone to the Science Center to see the train exhibit or to the mall to select a pair of the Marcasite earrings he always buys her for the holidays, Ma had probably been mailing the letter in the box outside the boutique where she works. Ma never misses a day selling dresses and accessories, not even to join her husband and daughter at play.

Exhausted, as if she had walked the six hundred miles rather than flown, Vera again collapses in her blue chair. She wraps her floral quilt around her, the same quilt that she slept in as a little girl and that still bears a small chocolate syrup stain in the middle of a blue flower. Just as the snow continues to assault the ground, so do Vera's memories continue to attack her. Seven days before her trip home, her panic intensified as excitement and anxiety began their usual battle within her. She longed to run off the plane into the welcoming arms of Dad, but she feared the scrutiny of General Mother. Every day after school, before she shed her classroom clothes for extra-large sweats, Vera would stand before her closet, trying to choose the perfect traveling outfit that would earn kudos from Ma and set a positive tone for the rest of the visit. Only an hour before leaving for the airport did she finally decide upon a navy-blue knee-length skirt with a matching vest. To add some flair to the ensemble, she chose a red, white, and blue long-sleeved blouse with a bow, blue flats, and blue fishnet stockings. Yet, even as Vera dressed, she knew the General would find some fault. She just never anticipated it would take the form of a venomous letter written in angry blue ink.

That blue outfit you wore was very unbecoming, Ma scrawled across the page. *It made you look like a barrel covered in blue wrapping paper. And those stockings just brought attention to your thick legs and swollen ankles! What were you thinking?*

The wind howls like sobs through Vera's closed window. She pretends that Mother Nature is extending sympathy towards her, but she knows better. Vera knows she is as alone as that isolated person she sees crossing the street, his head bent forward in an attempt to push away the snow that pelts against his face. She wonders why he is out on such a night, especially when she sees that he is wearing regular shoes, not the boots that the storm requires. The blizzard probably caught him unaware—just like Ma's letter caught *her* off guard.

Vera turns away from the window and man of snow, searching her apartment for some kind of comfort. The poster of Freud hanging above her couch/bed seems to mock her more than appease her. "Vat do you expect?" she hears the good doctor ask. "If you eat ice cream, do you tink you vill be skinny? Even if you eat nothing, do you tink *Irhe Mutter* vill praise you?" Vera turns to the poster of Shakespeare, the only other wall decoration, for support, but Big Bill for once seems speechless. No sounds come out of the Bard's mouth, and the hand holding his quill pen does not move.

Unwrapping herself from her quilt, Vera again hoists her bulk off the chair, places the letter on the round kitchen table, and heads for the bathroom. Maybe a hot shower will melt away her fat and her thoughts. She closes the bathroom door, a habit from her youth when she needed to protect her modesty in a house occupied by an intrusive mother and an annoying older brother, and turns on the hot water faucet almost to scalding. As she scrubs her body, she keeps her eyes closed. It is one thing to feel her flesh, but a totally different matter to see it.

Once out of the shower, though, Vera feels a masochistic desire to examine the body that causes her—and Ma—so much sadness and disappointment. She stands before the mirror attached to the back of the bathroom door. Vera, who perceives mirrors as the enemy, would never have chosen to have one in her apartment. When she discovered this one, a leftover from the previous tenant, she vowed to remove it but never got around to doing so. Now, staring into its steamy surface, she feels some sort of sick pleasure at knowing the power that it holds. Vera takes a dry wash cloth and slowly wipes away the steam from the top—just enough to reveal her wet hair and damp face. She scrutinizes her long face, convinced that since reading the letter, her cheeks and chin have that swollen look she gets from bee stings.

Like a surgeon peeling away layer after layer of skin and muscle to reach the core of the problem, Vera wipes off a bit more of the steam to reveal a collar bone that no longer juts out and sagging breasts that seem to have lost their perkiness. She continues to wipe, helped by the cooler air that speeds up the process, until enough of the mirror opens to reflect Vera's belly—a bloated, fleshy container of newly-digested vanilla ice cream.

Eager to bring this painful unveiling to an end, Vera swipes the wash cloth against the bottom half of the mirror. At last she sees her 5-feet, 8-inch body in all its naked imperfection: a raisin-shaped mole darkening the skin above her left breast; a wide scar, a souvenir from ovarian surgery five years earlier, snaking from her belly button, wiggling south, and disappearing in her grassy pubic hair; and a maze of freckles creating an irregular connect-the-dots game on both her legs.

This is what Vera's mirror shows her, but Vera knows that Ma's mirror is even more potent. It is the distorted mirror found in a fun house, the one that acts like a garbage compactor by compressing Vera until her head seems to sprout from her waist and her body seems to expand to twice its size. Vera sees herself through the mirror of Ma's eyes—a linebacker built for blocking all opponents except a mother whose disappointment and disapproval rush at her, tackle her, and leave her lying face down in the dirt.

Vera slams the open door against the wall, hoping to shatter the mirror. Her failure makes her feel frenzied, almost as if she needs more self-inflicted pain before she can release herself from the pain of the letter's blue words. She opens her medicine cabinet, silently praying that its two dried-up bottles of nail polish, squeezed-from-the-top tube of toothpaste, and waxy container of deodorant will magically transform into containers of pills and capsules that will forever end that emptiness that consumes her.

When prayer and magic fail her, Vera searches the bathroom for something else—for anything—to alleviate her anxiety. Instead, she sees the silver scale tucked beneath the sink. Vera rarely uses the scale, a moving-in gift from Ma, but now she pulls it out with her foot. As she steps on it, the dust from its surface clings to her wet soles. Like a statistician analyzing her data, Vera studies the numbers as they rapidly increase under her weight: 50, 75, 100, 125, 145, 155, 156, 157. One hundred and fifty-seven pounds. Not enough to get her a job as the Fat Lady at the circus, but more than enough to motivate Ma to write, *You look like the Fat Lady at the circus.*

Vera has had enough—enough of scales, mirrors, blue words, Ma. She quickly dresses in her flannel pajamas, the pink ones with lace around the collar and sleeves that make her feel like Wendy in *Peter Pan*, and heads to the kitchen to make a hot cup of Ovaltine, Dad's panacea for all ills.

"Dad, no one asked me to dance at the school party. Then, the teacher made Freddy, the shortest boy in the class, ask me. His head only reached my belly button!"

"Have some Ovaltine, honey. It will help you see the humor in this!"

"Dad, everyone is going to the prom but me. I'll be the only one without a corsage and long dress. I feel like Cinderella when her stepsisters left her behind to go to the ball!"

"Let me make us some Ovaltine, sweetie. Then let's play some Scrabble. Maybe you'll give your old Dad a chance and let me win for a change!"

If only it were that simple, Vera sighs as she heats up the Ovaltine. She uses skim milk, but then adds about ten miniature marshmallows to the drink. Carefully holding her M&M's mug, she walks to her blue chair and once again squeezes into it. The marshmallows coat her mouth with a sweet fluffiness, almost as if she were eating a chocolate-covered cloud.

As she slowly sips, Vera rests her forehead against the window and looks at the park across the street. A group of undergraduates, all dressed in the purple and blue colors of the local university, are celebrating New Year's Eve with a snowball fight. One girl, her long blonde hair looking almost white in the storm, leaps onto the back of a guy who has to be a football player. Not even her bulky clothes or his icy shoulders cause her a problem. Vera, watching this acrobatic feat, admires the curves of the girl's perfectly shaped body that her thick winter coat cannot camouflage.

Apparently tiring of their escapades, the kids decide to build a snowman. Working in groups of two or three, they gather snow and begin rolling it into a big ball. Vera remembers how Grandma would take a small ball of flour, add to it, and keep rolling and adding until she had enough dough to flatten for her pie crust. The tantalizing aroma of cinnamon apple pie fills Vera with nostalgia; she wishes she could again be that little girl who spent one New Year's Eve eating corned beef sandwiches with Grandma and learning how to play Canasta.

Vera watches as the college students add layers to the snowman. Her eyes follow football guy as he rolls two separate balls and, much to the delight of his comrades, slams them into the snowman's chest. He then grabs Blonde Barbie around her waist, lifts her off the ground, and twirls her. The scene reminds Vera of the jewelry box with its dancing ballerina that Grandma had bought her when she turned ten. After the girls honor Snow Woman with a curtsy and the boys kiss her nonexistent lips, they dash off to some fraternity house where they will officially welcome the New Year.

For the next hours, long after the old year has melted into the New Year, Vera stays in her blue chair and looks at Snow Woman. She stares at her lopsided, sagging breasts and the piece of dirt that looks like a mole above her left breast. The wind blows a loose twig onto Snow Woman's abdomen. It reminds Vera of an imperfect surgical scar. As the snow adds inches to Snow Woman's head and stomach and thighs, Vera begins to sweat and gasp for breath. The arms of the blue chair seem to close around her in a suffocating hug. Then, as if the Ovaltine has injected too much caffeine into her veins, Vera jumps from her blue chair, grabs a plastic shopping bag she keeps under the sink, and fills the bag with what she needs. She doesn't even bother to get dressed, but instead slips her blue winter coat over her pajamas. She barely remembers to put on socks before donning her blue boots. With bag in hand, she rushes down the steps.

Vera thrusts two Oreo cookies onto Snow Woman's face, giving her dark eyes that look like overly-dilated pupils in a constant state of surprise or shock. With a chocolate candy bar, Vera creates a wide, horizontal nose that has no openings for air. A handful of M&M's yields a colorful but melancholy smile, while long pieces of chocolate licorice add spidery eyebrows and porcupine-like hair. Vera places the empty vanilla ice cream carton onto Snow Woman's spiky hair and turns its flaps into ear muffs to protect her glazed doughnut ears from the intense wind. Finally, she takes her rumpled blue fishnet pantyhose, the same stockings that caused Ma such grief, and wraps them around Snow Woman's neck. Vera stretches the nylons so that each foot discreetly covers each of Snow Woman's breasts. After giving her snowy clone an awkward but affectionate hug, Vera returns to her apartment and the blue chair by the window.

Neither Vera nor Snow Woman react to the cacophony of noisemakers or the explosion of fireworks that continues long after midnight. Neither pays attention to the heavy snow that threatens to bury Snow Woman. Instead, Vera and Snow Woman use Vera's steamy window as an Etch-a-Sketch to play games of Tic-Tac-Toe and Hangman. They try to write a return letter to Ma, but by the time Vera finishes the salutation and "got your letter" beginning, she runs out of space on her glass paper.

Although Vera fears falling asleep and leaving Snow Woman vulnerable to the bullying of nature and late-night revelers, she eventually closes her eyes. She does not see Snow Woman's breasts collapse under the weight of the snow and fall to the ground, creating a puddle of milky whiteness. She does not see a lone drunk steal Snow Woman's M&M's smile. Only when the sun invades her apartment does Vera awaken. She sits listlessly in her blue chair, watching as the sun's rays cast a spotlight upon the dust balls hiding in corners, the piles of crumbs waiting for a family of hungry ants, and the waste basket overflowing with candy wrappers. When the sun extends its bony arms to the letter sitting on the kitchen table, Vera wraps the quilt tightly around her, wishing she could stay in her cocoon forever.

Vera does not yet realize that the sun has melted Snow Woman into a white corpse. A pair of fishnet stockings—the same blue as Ma's words—serves as her shroud.

About the Author:

Ronna is a daughter and mother, a teacher and student, a reader and writer. Although she has traveled extensively, she welcomes spending her "golden years" in Pittsburgh, the city of her birth. Ronna begins each day at the gym, only exercising on machines that allow her to read as she works out. Most of her days end at one of the city's many theatres where she volunteers as an usher, or in the home of one of the many middle school/high school students she tutors. As a part-time faculty member of the University of Pittsburgh's English Department, Ronna works as a consultant at the Writing Center. She also has the pleasure of teaching Freshman Programs, a one-credit course that introduces students new to Pitt to the rich opportunities of both the University and the city. Despite her busy schedule, Ronna always finds time to spend with her close friend and roommate—her 93-year-old father.

"I thank Dad for teaching me that a cold chocolate phosphate in the summer and a hot cup of Ovaltine in the winter can ease all problems, Jonathan and Ilana for reminding me that the past does not have to define the present or the future, and Ma for allowing me to make real her teaching and writing dreams."

THIRD PLACE

A WRETCHED AND NOBLE DAY
©2010 by Frederic H. Decker

A wretched day for standing in line—nearly an hour so far for Bert, advancing forward ever so slowly, massed together involuntarily with persons unknown, persons there for a similar purpose but unknown nonetheless. And persons who were sweating. It was difficult not to sweat. Without a doubt, an unusually hot and humid day. Several weeks before the official summer beginning and already there was ninety-one degrees and a humidity percentage over eighty. The air was oppressive and heavy in the lungs when inhaled, as if layers of cotton obstructed the ready penetration of the spongy membrane. This place was also an old building and the state government could never convince itself to spend money to install central air conditioning. And what window units there were...well, they did nothing for the stairwells and hallways in which Bert and others waited.

Sweat from Bert's armpits had soaked through his shirt, and patches of moisture were beginning to appear through the back. Bert was only halfway up the first flight of stairs with another flight of line still remaining between him and what he hoped was the door to the Office of Income Maintenance. Having never been here before, Bert had no knowledge of what actually awaited him past that door. He only hoped for no more line, no more squeezing and crowding for position on the steps. He hoped for more air.

He also hoped his present unemployment was not a telling prophecy of what his life would be. Right now, the notion of a stable career was hard to imagine and outside the boundaries of the touchable, despite the repeated times Bert told himself that he was only a few years out of college and just starting life's journey— assuming the average life expectancy was his to have. Still, getting laid off from work was a first, making the future of what life really offered a person very uncertain and questionable. Today, finding temporary work was as worthy a future as any Bert could imagine. But today even temporary work was evasive.

Only two or three minutes had passed since Bert last moved up a step closer to his destiny with the Office of Income Maintenance, but the irritation of sweat made it feel ten times longer. Despite the annoyance, Bert tried to remain calm with no purpose served by getting aroused and letting this ordeal get to him since, upset or not, the wait would take the same time. Best to simply stand there silent and irritated. Even his private internal discourse—often entertaining, often magical in conclusion, often carried on at a fast pace—had slowed down and was nearly a blank. Sweat finally reached Bert's eyes and, with his handkerchief out, he rubbed them trying to wipe the stinging away. Then he wiped off his brow.

"Who ya think ya are?" said the middle-aged stout woman standing behind Bert, causing Bert to turn around thinking the woman was speaking to him. It was not him, rather a young woman with a child in her arms pushing her way up the worn wooden stairs, maneuvering in the center where the concave path left by the many she joined marked a clear line to the top.

"I got'n appointment. Going to check in," responded the young woman climbing up the stairs with evident determination, brushing up against and past the people standing in line on the steps until she reached the step on which Bert stood. Then suddenly she moved to the side toward Bert, holding her child more firmly and turning her back to the center of the stairway. She was getting out of the way of the towering woman walking down the stairs in a rude rush to exit, giving no attention to anyone in the path of her descent, not even to the young woman with child in arms.

Moving with the shuffling of bodies, Bert found himself pressed up against the wall. Yet, even after, Bert still had no commentary, not even privately to himself. None about the void of enjoyment this wait in line possessed, nothing about his struggle to rebound from the wall and regain his rightful place on the steps; only merely wondering if, instead of this dutiful wait, maybe he too could have made an appointment like that woman with the child.

The woman continued the ascent of the stairway with her child in arms leaving Bert standing behind. But, however slowly, as the lead of the line before him moved farther up away from the open entrance door, Bert followed in the climb where the air became more still and stale. "Free sauna while you wait," said Bert. He chuckled over the idea to the woman behind him who gave Bert a faint, polite smile with no comprehension of Bert's banter. Growing more restless, Bert shuffled his feet while standing in place on the step.

When finally reaching the doorway on the second floor about a half of an hour later, Bert read the sign commanding: *Please Wait Here Until Called Next*. There beyond the sign stood two persons behind a counter whom Bert recognized immediately as the gatekeepers between him and whomever he really needed to see. Off to the left of the counter were six rows of metal folding chairs. The walls were dirt-ridden, previously a uniform tan but on this day, as recent yesterdays, spotted with uneven hue. Bert couldn't resist feeling dirty himself as he surveyed the room.

Bert saw the young woman with her baby sitting in the second row of chairs, apparently waiting for that appointment. Next to the woman sat a male about Bert's age wearing a white shirt and a subtly striped tie. Seeing this guy was unexpected. Bert didn't know what to expect, exactly, but this guy was never in anything Bert pictured.

Now Bert began to question his own attire. Not wearing a tie was intentional: Bert not wanting to appear anything close to well-tailored. He was working-class and none other. No white collar was to be found around his neck. But now? He wondered. Was his choice of apparel a mistake? If his own case was borderline—which he feared—would wearing a tie, being more formal and business-like, have helped him forge an impression to push his case into favorable judgment? *Ridiculous*, Bert thought. Really, how could a tie be important or useful here? Besides, that guy's shirt was as moist from sweat as Bert's, or anyone else's. Still, when Bert heard the loud announcement, "Next," the uncertainty of his dress dissolved what confidence he had manufactured for the day as he walked up to the counter.

"How can I help you?" The woman's smile seemed out of place. Too welcoming. Too dignified. Even the perspiration Bert noticed under her arms appeared unlike his own.

Bert felt unprepared before her. He grew embarrassed. "I, uh...I'm applying for food stamps."

"Are you currently receiving food stamps?"

With emphasis, capturing a brief moment of clarity, Bert answered, "No. That's why I'm here. I want to apply for stamps." For whatever reason, of which Bert had no clue, the woman looked clearly annoyed by his answer. Embarrassment deepened and rushed fully to the surface of Bert's face. The warmth added more sweat.

"What I mean is this isn't a re-application for another allocation?"

Hearing the firmness in the woman's question, with a certain message behind it, Bert now wished more than before to please, tempering his reply accordingly: "Sorry. This is the first time I've been here."

"What's your name?"

"Bert Nichols."

"Have a seat and I'll *have* someone see you. It'll be about fifteen minutes." The woman finished writing Bert's name on the waiting list.

No longer did the woman seem out of place. No longer was she too dignified for the surroundings. Only the typical common in nightmares. *Right, she will "have" someone see me. As if she is the All-powerful One.* As the satisfaction of his private rebuttal faded and turned to meaning little, Bert walked back to a chair and sat in the row behind the one where the young woman and baby had been sitting. They were no longer there, apparently at *that* appointment.

Bert glanced over at the young woman sitting in the next chair. Their eyes met. A man then came out of the hallway and stood before Bert and the others waiting for their name. "Mr. Reed," the man called out. The tie-clad guy rose and followed his potential state-financed patron down the hallway, disappearing into that unknown for which Bert waited. Bert looked away and stared at the picture on the wall in front of him, the picture of the secretary of the Department of Human Services above the State's seal of the Department, the patron saint of all gathered in this room. The image was less than holy hanging on the dirty walls and Bert gained no encouragement from it.

Bert sat there thinking about how no one he knew ever needed to do what he was doing (as far as he knew). More to the point: Through a lot of his life he had come to think, as probably did many others, that people who got the benefits of dole, people like those with whom he presently sat, were different people. They were a different breed among themselves, cattle for whom the best that could be hoped for was that they stayed herded up in their separate pasture until butchered by the slaughterhouse of their own vices. Today, however, no one in the room seemed different to Bert. Some likely had been here before, more familiar with the process, but Bert didn't think they were different. If anything, he was the outsider wanting to know what he needed to do to belong.

Twenty minutes later, Bert heard the announcement, "Mr. Nichols," and he was up and shaking hands in good speed, oblivious to the sweat on his forehead and that staining his shirt under his arms.

"Hi, I'm Tom Daniel. Let's go into my office." Daniel pointed down the hall to his closed office door.

So, this was the person Bert really had to see. Tom Daniel couldn't have been much older than himself, if older at all, Bert surmised. And then there was Daniel's apparel: a blue and white checkered short-sleeved shirt with a darker blue tie with no appearance of sweat. The lack of sweat struck Bert as peculiar. How could this guy not be sweating buckets through his shirt? No common experience with Daniel was felt shared even though Daniel was about the same age as Bert. No similar worlds joined in their handshake.

Chilliness came over Bert when entering Daniel's office, quick and unexpected, marked by skin tightened in defense as the coolness from the window air conditioning unit hit his damp shirt. Hairs on Bert's arms stood more erect, for that moment, then rested at ease, the cool air now welcomed.

Moving past Bert, Daniel placed the legal-sized application form in front of him while he sat behind his desk and forewent any further niceties of conversation before getting down to business: "Do you have some type of identification I can use to copy off your name and address? Your driver's license is fine."

Bert's attention heightened. His heart pulsated in anxious anticipation. The moment was *here.* Bert pulled his license from his wallet and gave it to Daniel in a movement laced with the feeling that the validity of his whole existence was now passing between hands, into the control of another's hands.

Daniel copied the name and birth date from the license. "Is this still your address?"

"Yes."

"Do you live alone?"

Bert nodded yes.

The inquiry continued: "And do you have a home phone number?"

Now a conclusion of abuse dominated Bert's words as he recited his phone number, fully mindful at the same time of his susceptibility, a weakness, in having his fate—or at least some of his immediate material means—dependent on another person's decision-making (and by inference, another person's degree of competence). This position, this feeling closing in on an unwelcome dependency, was exacerbated by Daniel's probing style requiring, maybe even demanding, Bert's presence as the passive vehicle of information only. Bert wanted to grab back the beginning when he handed over his driver's license. He wanted to say something on his own, but with fear's hesitation, the words forming within were kept to himself: *Why don't you ask me why I'm here or what I need, you idiot?*

"Oh!" Daniel said, realizing an oversight. "How long have you lived at your current address?"

"About two years," Bert replied simply, masking as best he could the enragement that, up from his stomach and chest cavity, crept to the surface of his skin and down his arms and legs, driven out by the pounding rhythm, by the erupting vibration in the singularity of the monotone syllables heard and spoken. He moved in his seat. His answers were numbers for a bingo game thrown into a bowl to be shaken and rattled and drawn to see what was revealed. If he was lucky, he would hear Daniel yell "Bingo!"

He could not take a chance of offending this guy sitting on the other side of the desk, but with the surfacing energy more than should be hidden, out it came: "I'm here to see if I can get food stamps!" The outburst petered out in its verbalization. Only Bert felt threatened by what he said. Only to Bert was the outburst meant to shake things up.

"Yes, yes, I know that," Daniel acknowledged, obviously unaware of any problem, with the reason for Bert's visit written next to his name by Ms. Riverfield, the woman behind the counter who had put Bert's name on the waiting list. Moving down the form to the next line, Daniel continued, "You own or rent where you live?"

"Rent."

"Do you have a receipt from your last rent payment?"

Bert handed Daniel the cancelled check he brought with him, wondering if he paid enough or too little or too much. Who knew? Bert didn't. He knew nothing about the fine print in the rule book of dole-getting.

"Are you employed right now, Mr. Nichols?"

"No."

"What was your last job, then?"

With all his rehearsals for his answer to this question, Bert had prepared a tale which sounded reasonable and whatever other adjectives applied to a world of rationality. But now all those adjectives felt elsewhere. "I, uh, was working, uh, as a drywall finisher's helper on that shopping mall built on West Boulevard. Job ended and laid off. And, uh, haven't been many new construction jobs around. Not much building being done nowadays, you know." *Damn it,* Bert thought, wondering if he rambled on too much about his drywall job.

"Recently laid off, then."

"About a month ago."

"You filed for unemployment?"

"Just received my last unemployment check this month."

"What? It's only been a month." Knowing something about unemployment eligibility and benefits, Daniel knew that what Bert said did not fit.

"Right, I, uh...the construction job was for only three months. Before that I was collecting unemployment for the job I had before where I was first laid off."

"I see. Go on. What was that?"

"A research assistant in a study for the state, evaluating drug treatment programs." Bert's first job out of college with his degree in criminal justice. "It was a job for eighteen months coding data that was collected. I was told there might be more work but the grant funding didn't happen, I was told."

"And that was when, that you were laid off there?"

"About eleven months ago. When I got temporary jobs, I didn't collect the unemployment. Stretched out my benefits."

"What did you do in between. How did you 'stretch' it out. You can't do that today?"

Now with the unspoken charge made public, Bert was surrounded with the accusation that he wasn't trying hard enough. Now blamed, he was losing and would be kept from the assistance for which he came. Hesitation to tell all was not wise, Bert having to make sure Daniel understood his effort and the many temporary jobs he had worked. Bert went on telling about the temp agency that occasionally found Bert work in an office doing clerical work such as stuffing envelopes for mass mailings, filing, and answering phones, and sometimes jobs the agency called "light industrial." But the agency had nothing right now for Bert. Nothing. A cornered, frightened dog, barking loudly to be heard, would recognize Bert's predicament as he told his story.

"Nothing available now? So, you haven't been able to find anything, huh? How about the state again? Being near the capital, there may be opportunities there worth investigating. Many state buildings right here in Hillsborough." Daniel genuinely thought he was giving helpful advice.

"Yes, sir, I've applied to some state jobs," Bert blurted out in his defense. "Taken some state exams, too. Applied for other positions. Can't even find a restaurant who needs a waiter or something, and I've gone to every restaurant in town I know of, more than once." Bert was now beginning to question himself. Should he be working somewhere? He was trying everything, he thought, but having to explain it all to Daniel made Bert feel otherwise at the moment, as if all his attempts to find a job counted for little.

"Uh-huh," Daniel mumbled. "Do you have a checking or savings account, Bert?"

"A checking account."

"How much is in your checking account?"

"About three hundred dollars. Don't know exactly."

"You're allowed to have that much. We'll need a statement from your bank to certify the amount."

Quietly, Bert sighed in relief. He was poor enough to make it.

With questions completed for this case, Daniel turned to the representation of Bert's existence he had scribbled onto the application form and jotted down his notes on the dole available for Bert that he considered fair, a minimum amount per month for three months with purpose being to hold Bert over for a while.

"I see, for three months," Bert said after hearing what he was to get.

"Yes. You'll need to reapply for coupons after that if your situation has not changed. The coupons will be mailed to you."

"They'll be mailed?"

"Yes."

Not having to come down and stand in line for his food stamps brought Bert an unanticipated closure he welcomed, welcomed until the possibilities of folly set in and Bert feared bureaucratic bungling could be reasons nothing would ultimately show up in the mail, all lost in the heap of the unfortunate, like having a patron saint lay down one's wager in craps—a free throw at the table—but without hands to throw the dice, the arms having been amputated. Bert took a large swallow and, expressing his lingering distrust, asked: "The application has to be approved or processed by somebody else?"

"It has to be processed with my approval. You'll get your coupons. You do need to send the verification from your bank before I can process anything." Daniel handed Bert a self-addressed envelope for him to use.

Bert left Daniel's office, headed down the stairs, got into his car, and drove off to the bank.

The wind ran through the open car windows, rearranging Bert's hair and drying the sticky perspiration that had grown in volume and more uncomfortable while waiting in the heat at the last red light. Bert's car was an old, reliable Dodge Dart without air conditioning. So, Bert's shirt fell deeper into sweat's obliteration. He should head home to replace this faulty apparel, but there was no real time with closing hour near and waiting until tomorrow unsatisfactory. That bank verification was wanted today, *now* in Daniel's hand, and a second's delay was too much. Bert unbuttoned his shirt to allow the wind's entrance and the shirt began to dry. Still clinging to the steering wheel, Bert lifted his arms to also allow the air to cool the hair drowning in his armpits.

As the bank drew nearer, the grip of Bert's hands weakened, trembling slightly in their hold on the steering wheel, while his left leg shook noticeably when he pushed down on the clutch pedal to shift gears. He was being overtaken. Bert inhaled deeply and slowly several times trying to relax himself. The controlled breathing helped some. Perplexing was this sudden flood of emotion. Never was Bert overcome like this when receiving unemployment money. As he learned, he was able to get unemployment checks because he had been employed long enough to be covered by the unemployment insurance. He did not have to demonstrate anything else other than he had been productive sufficiently to warrant his share of help. Now, however, he had to demonstrate that he was poor. Before it was just between him and the personnel at the unemployment insurance office.

A traffic light sprang into Bert's awareness, prompting quick but barely coherent thoughts: *The light is red. How long has it been red? Who cares how long, slam on the brakes!* Stopped five feet past the crosswalk, Bert encountered the disapproval and contempt packaged in the glare from the driver who had to swirl around him. Bert backed the car a few feet.

The shock of impending disaster diverted his thoughts more, further than breathing only, ironically more calming, frightening him out of the confusion that had sprung up from his indulgence in pride. Remaining focused and calm, Bert turned into the bank's parking lot. But once parked and out of the car walking toward the entrance of the bank, the specter of humiliation once again embraced Bert. Another deep breath was taken when Bert opened the bank door and entered the cinder-block building housing and symbolizing monetary stability and wealth.

The walls were a clean and strong medium blue. Off in the corner the waiting area was neatly arranged with padded benches against the walls accompanied by plants growing out of their pots resting on the floor. The bank representatives on duty were with clients at their desks. No one else was waiting. Bert would be next.

The wait was preparing. Bert encouraged himself to be firm, not to be cowed, not to be timid when facing one of those bank representatives. He needed to tell them what he *wanted* point blank without the hesitation of a waffling fruitcake. They needed to know that he had to have a letter from them documenting the amount in his account *today*, in his hand before he left the bank. Rude impatience would be his display if anyone suggested that he would have to come back tomorrow for the final letter. The picture had to be made clear: Absolutely no room for negotiation. Hardball was the necessary game with these financial giants, with these pillars of respectability. They weren't going to get up on a higher-than-thou horse and treat him as a disreputable person in society who had no more business for their bank. He wouldn't let them. Respect was going to be shown to *him*.

Bert was armed and ready when signaled by the woman behind the desk closest to him that he was next. Bert passed the man who had just completed his business with the woman and walked up to the chair in front of the desk and before his buttock even touched the chair he was explaining the action he required at an accelerated, hyperactive rate.

The woman listened attentively and then plainly stated, "No problem." No visible expression of disbelief, dismay, or condescension was apparent. She paused to introduce herself: "My name is Ruth Roland. And you are?"

"Oh, yes...I just started talking, didn't I? Bert Nichols."

Bert felt comfort in Ruth Roland's matter-of-fact response and surrendered himself to her actions. If he could only take her home with him, that is, take home the security presently felt in her presence. If she could only be there always, as she was now, to mother him, to hold him in her arms with his head resting against her breast, telling him that it was all right and everything would work out. Comfort along this line Bert felt from Ruth Roland. This security, so pleasurable and warm, Bert would welcome (with the touch of mammary glands pressed against his ear) in place of actually shrinking at this moment and climbing into the moist protection of her womb.

Ruth keyed in Bert's name on the computer terminal. "Your address and phone number?" Ruth asked to verify that the correct account number was on the monitor screen. Bert's answer fit, so Ruth scribbled the account balance down on the note pad.

"Let me get this letter typed and I'll bring it over to you. You can have a seat over there if you like." Ruth pointed to the waiting area.

A short time later, Ruth went over to Bert with the signed letter in hand for Bert to read. "Is it all you need?" she asked.

Bert read the note hoping it was all he needed. "That probably is good enough," Bert stated. He could finally go home.

On the way home from the bank, Bert had stopped off and mailed the letter to Tom Daniel. Ruth Roland was kind enough to make a photocopy of the letter for Bert's records before he left. Hand-delivering the letter to Daniel was preferred, obviously not wanting to chance its loss through the mail, but it was near the close of Daniel's—and others'—workday. Moreover, Bert was tired and low on the daily supply of inspiration needed to face again that line of unpredictable waiting. Thus weary, Bert trusted others with his fate, which was not an easy thing for him to do. No letter Bert ever mailed had been lost as far as he knew, but this time dropping his banker's letter into that levered opening of the postal box was like a drop into a dark abyss. Bert opened and closed the levered lid three times to assure himself that the letter had dropped in safely—a compulsive act that, however much felt as a strong demand, was no replacement for, was not as good as, handing the letter to Daniel directly. In a couple of days, he would call Daniel to make sure the bank letter arrived and everything was being processed as told.

Upon entering his apartment, springing up from where Bert could not say, joy seized him and he giggled and wriggled his hips in a dance of triumph over the day's opposing forces. He laughed. "I'm on food stamps!" he shouted, laughing even louder. After that he sat in the chair nearest the door and stared at the wall with a concentration only known to those with nothing on which to concentrate.

Going to the Office of Income Maintenance wasn't as bad as Bert thought it would be. Well, standing in line was a little abrasive, and answering all the questions was a bit, well, *more than a bit*, humiliating. But Bert felt pretty comfortable now having made it through. The time he wasted in thinking about applying for food stamps, the hesitation to acknowledge that he was at a place where food stamps made sense. Now with the ordeal completed, now having done what he needed to do for himself, Bert knew that applying for food stamps was reasonable and, yes, courageous.

And maybe even noble.

About the author:

Frederic H. Decker spent his formative years from high school through college in Florida. Before that he spent most of his youth in his birthplace, Cincinnati. Despite his Midwestern roots, he is told he has some Southern tones in his voice. Today Frederic lives in Bowie, Maryland where he is able to enjoy sailing on the nearby Chesapeake Bay. Educated as a sociologist at Florida State University, he has published research through the years in academic journals. "A Wretched and Noble Day" is his first published fiction. He is pleased he can now say more "officially" that he is a fiction writer. He has other short stories and two novels in the works to add to his list of fiction writing.

~HONORABLE MENTION~

MY 'IRISH' FATHER
©2010 by Dan Sullivan

Whenever I'm introduced, it's obvious that I'm Irish, or more precisely, an American of Irish descent. Besides the name—Kevin Michael Kilgarriff—the freckles and the red hair are dead giveaways. The Kilgariffs of Bethesda, Maryland, however, are not your stereotypical Irish. Not your basic *I'll knock yer teeth out, fecker, if you keep muggin' me that way* Irish or *Have a wee drop or two of Bushmill's with me and we'll see who can drink the other under the table* Irish. We're not at all like our wild and windy ancestors from County Kerry who left there in the 1890s to escape hanging for treason—as family legend would have it—but more likely to evade arrest for petty theft. None of the Kilgariffs is a poet or a pugilist. None of us has the messianic fire of a liberator. None of us has even read James Joyce's *Ulysses* (and let's have a show of hands of how many English majors or even their professors who have *actually* read *Ulysses* cover to cover...I didn't think so). Not one of the Kilgariffs has ever chucked a Molotov cocktail in Londonderry or challenged Victor McLaglen of *The Quiet Man* fame to a fistfight, and surely none of us has ever *ever* missed Mass on Sundays—except maybe Brendan, the youngest and the family black sheep who abandoned us all five years ago and escaped to Seattle.

So contrary to what others probably assume when they first

43

hear our name, our "Irishness" comes not from the pub or the hanging tree, but the cloister. Nor did the Kilgariff scrupulosity, fastidiousness, and precision about religion stem from my mother's side of the family, the Gottschalks—a sensible and upright bunch of Germans who brought forth a tribe of perfectly logical and easy-going Lutherans. It was my father, Dan Kilgariff, who endowed us with those former traits. So throughout most of their marriage, my father and mother waged skirmishes over "all things Catholic": women priests, the Latin Mass, the authority of the Pope, the amount to be dropped in the Sunday collection basket, or whether their three children should attend Catholic school. Predictably, my father always sat on the right side of the aisle on a given religious issue while my mother naturally camped on the left. Their differences were always simmering just below the surface, and one evening they erupted when my mother blasted my father in a voice hoarse with rage, "You should have been a priest!"

That night, I prayed with all my heart that her outbreak was a comment not on Dad's lovemaking abilities but rather frustration of living with a man who was, as she said, "Hell-bent on being holier than the Pope."

So that was our grounding, and now, even as an adult, whenever I call Dad on Sundays, his first question to me is not, "How are you?" "How's your job or your love life?" but "What Mass did you go to?" I wouldn't say that my father drove my mother to an early grave, but Dad's temperament and fastidious approach to life and the Lord certainly didn't add any years to her life. After much retrospection, I believe that Ma was completely off base when she said that Dad should have been a priest, and I've told her so in prayers; I am now more convinced than ever that Dad should have been a nun.

I mentioned that we are the Kilgariffs of Bethesda, Maryland. That's *essentially* correct. Margaret Mary, the oldest, whose preferred attire is a black pants suit, lives two blocks away from Dad with her husband Chase, a nice enough guy floating on the margins of our family, who always seems to wear a baffled smile and whose only faults are that he was once a Presbyterian and is now married to Margaret Mary. (Brendan half-joked once that Chase *has* to be on controlled substances to be living with Margaret Mary.) Margaret Mary and Chase have a girl fourteen years old named Mary Margaret, who is in basic training to become a full-fledged Margaret Mary someday. (I get their names confused all the time myself.) Anyhow, my sister, Margaret Mary, is a devoted and loving daughter. I'll give her that. She looks in on Dad every day, does his grocery shopping and laundry, makes sure he takes his medicine on time, drives him to Sunday Mass, and calls at least twice daily. She also knows the number and location of every sterling spoon, every glass of Waterford crystal in Dad's house and has had her eye on Dad's Wedgewood china for years. Once, she and Mary Margaret refused to speak to me for six months after I had joked—admittedly after one shot too many of Bushmill's—that my sister needed to get a little color in her wardrobe because she looked like "a Mediterranean widow."

For my part, I live alone in an apartment about three miles from Dad and Margaret Mary—and of course Chase and Mary Margaret. And as I mentioned, only Brendan, my younger brother, dared to venture forth and escape Bethesda. And venture forth the lad did: to Seattle, about three thousand miles away, to pursue a career in law. *To pursue a career in law? Makes lots of sense, my fine young rebel, to run three thousand miles away as if Washington, D.C. didn't have enough work for a planet full of attorneys.* But who's kidding whom: we all really know why he relocated.

But if my candlepower weren't bright enough to figure it out on my own, Brendan wrote me within a year after his relocation, explaining it all.

October 2003
Dear Kevin:

I hope all is well. I never really explained my decision to take the job with the Pierce County Prosecutor's Office, although I suspect you know already. I just couldn't take it anymore. The whole scene with Dad and Margaret Mary was what psychologists call 'toxic.' Yes, I've been in therapy, and yes, it's helped a lot. And no, don't tell Dad because Margaret Mary will get wind of it and probably end up sending me an encyclical on the evils of psychotherapy since she read somewhere once that Freud had 'something to do with sex.' Speaking of Margaret Mary, what sin in what previous life, what past offense, what prior outrage, did poor old Chase commit to now be sentenced to a marriage with Margaret Mary? Doing hard time...life without the possibility of parole. Margaret Mary and Dad...the tag team champions of guilt. And the niece? I picture her dressed in mourning as well and sitting at the feet of the masters drinking in every word, studying every movement, learning every trick of the guilt trade. Maybe I never mentioned this before, it's so outrageous, but it was my sophomore year at Virginia Tech. I was home for Thanksgiving. You were in the living room with Dad. Chase and I were standing like useless schmucks in the kitchen. Margaret Mary had of course refused our offers of help with an aggravated "That's o.k." Then she proceeded to do the dishes herself—every movement accompanied by weary sighs and the heavy downbeat of saucepans on the stovetop, putting a price tag, as usual, on anything she ever did for anyone else. All the while the niece was off to the side taking mental notes. When Margaret Mary was finished "doing" the dishes, and Chase and I had bundled up all the trash, a task more worthy of our talents, she then laid out on the dining room table all the fine silverware and the Waterford crystal and proceeded to count and then recount every last piece. She then looked over at Dad, and in a stage whisper said, 'They're all here.'

'They're all here'? What in the name of all that is holy did she mean by that? 'They're all here.' What did they suspect? That America's Most Wanted—Chase—was stuffing the flatware in his pockets so he could feed some phantom drug problem? That I was pinching the stuff? Their suspicions certainly didn't surprise me. All throughout college, Dad seemed hell-bent on ferreting out of me with vague, circuitous questions whether I was gay or on drugs, a member of the Communist Party or attending weekly Mass. If he had asked me outright, I probably would have 'confessed' that I was in fact a gay card-carrying member of the Communist Party, who never went to Mass anymore and was considering conversion to Islam after I complete my Twelve-Step recovery work for a methamphetamine addiction. I would then of course have told Dad it was all a joke but he'd better keep the breakfront locked. But I suspect he would with a solemn face remind me of the dangers of even flirting with any form of apostasy, especially Islam.

Then just last month, Margaret Mary sent me a clipped note. No salutation, no warmth, no well wishes, nothing, just, 'I assume that you're settled. Please call Dad more often than you have been doing. If you can manage it, come back for a quick visit so that you can see with your own eyes how much he's aged in the last three months. His wall calendar remains at June, the month you left. MM.'

By the way, I have in fact seen Dad's wall calendar in the kitchen. It's scary. It does remain frozen at June 2003—and that was six years ago! To make matters even spookier, the artwork for June that year is a rendering of St. Monica pleading with her wayward son, Augustine, to turn his life around. My heart now goes out not only to Chase but also my baby brother Brendan who abandoned us all and broke our hearts to travel three thousand miles away to live in Seattle, *but that's o.k.* Returning to the letter....

Kevin, as I said, I just couldn't take it anymore so I left. It goes back a long way. When I was little—I guess this is therapeutic so please bear with me—I remember bouncing in to see Dad and bragged that I had just said a rosary. The six-year-old figured...rosary...Dad, this was bound to get me some serious props. Ruminating, however, Dad asked, 'Did you say the 'Hail Holy Queen' at the end? You haven't said the rosary until you've done that.'

I never said another one in my life after that, and whenever we had to say one at home, I just mumbled the words and thought about Jayne Mansfield. I remember also my first year in high school. I had been elected class treasurer. I came home and gave the glad tidings to Ma and Dad. Ma gave me this big, warm smile and said that it was wonderful. Dad gave his reluctant little half-smile and said that it was 'great' but maybe next time I could be elected president, and wouldn't that be nice? I never ran again for anything after that.

Kind of like my writing. In my junior year of high school, before Ma died, I announced that I had decided to become a writer. Before Ma could say a word of encouragement, Dad warned of the difficulties most writers have making ends meet. I never wrote any fiction after that, either.

But that's all old, unhappy stuff. On to the new good stuff. Big secret: I am living with a terrific woman. Her name is Valerie Cho. She works in the Pierce County Medical Examiner's Office. Kind of quick, I guess, for moving in together, but she's funny and good-natured and so honest and straightforward that she doesn't know how to be subtle. She's direct and practical and focused on the issue at hand, sometimes a little too blunt for Kilgariff tastes, I suspect, but the type of person you'd want to run a business or a rescue unit. Did I just write rescue unit? I just saw that in print... it's quite telling isn't it? Anyway, here's our picture. I'm the tall one. We're obviously not the best-looking couple on the runway, but we'll take each other. I know Ma would have liked her.

I studied the photo of a smiling Brendan with an Asian woman probably in her twenties, standing not too much higher than his waist, holding his hand and laughing without restraint. They're happy. Great for Brendan and Valerie! A Chinese-American Kilgariff? Not so great for Dad and Margaret Mary. Brendan then closed his letter with an invitation for me to come west for a visit. He sounded so young and eager that it touched my heart:

Seriously, you'd love it out here. We have plenty of room. Great coffee shops and unbeatable seafood. Puget Sound is gorgeous. There's a Catholic church within walking distance from our apartment building. And by the way, Michael, what Mass did you go to last Sunday?

I miss you,
  Brendan

And for several more years Brendan lived his life in Seattle with Valerie, punctuated by one lone visit "home" when he brought Valerie to meet the family, but that meeting and Margaret Mary's emergency room visit for heart palpitations, are stuff for the epic I'm drafting. Stay tuned.

The long and short of their visit is that the following month I flew to Seattle to be his best man. Instead of a bachelor party the night before the wedding, Valerie, her sister Roslyn, Brendan, and myself played canasta in their apartment until three in the morning. The wedding was at 10:30 a.m. in the Chinese Christian Church of Seattle, the Reverend Leon Tsu presiding. Roslyn, first violinist with the Seattle Symphony Orchestra, played an air from Bach, four lovely cousin bridesmaids in traditional Chinese floor-length silk gowns led the father of the bride and the future Mrs. Brendan Kilgariff down the aisle. The bride, of course, wore red. Dad and Margaret Mary and Mary Margaret naturally couldn't make it, and Chase was told not to.

But in spite of all this, miracle of miracles, the minor planets continued to orbit near the sun in Bethesda while one star shone far off in the western sky. This continued for a year or so until Dad started to decline. So as if on cue, on Dad's seventy-fifth birthday, the blackouts started—really serious, no-laughing-matter stuff for an old man with brittle bones, a stubborn streak, and a drive to make everyone in the universe feel sorry for him. His second heart attack sent him to specialists at Georgetown University Hospital, and soon after that, in 2009, the family vigils began. For the first one, all the Kilgariffs and the priest on call, one of the many Dad was friendly with, were summoned by Margaret Mary to the hospital with words dressed in black, "This may be Dad's final hours."

That night, we found Dad ashen, "unanointed," and uncommunicative, presumably close to the end. (His priest on call, on that occasion, an affable young Franciscan, had completely screwed up and went to the wrong hospital. He would later be dropped from Dad's elite roster of "Priests on Call.") As for the Kilgariffs, all present and accounted for on *the first night,* except for Brendan and Valerie.

When Brendan and Valerie finally did arrive close to the end of visiting hours *on the second night* of that first family vigil, they squeezed through a packed hospital room with a plant that at one point in its existence may have seen water and fertilizer. I waved from the other side of the room, and the others shifted uncomfortably as Brendan and Valerie approached Dad. The room sounded as if they had invaded the silence of the British Museum, come late for Solemn High Mass celebrated by the Archbishop himself, or whistled past a coffin.

Margaret Mary, standing at the head of Dad's bed, looked at the floor, and Dad with averted eyes and a wan smile said only, "That's OK, Brendan."

Brendan seemed to regress and actually become smaller in front of us. *The incredible shrinking brother.* He immediately launched into an elaborate and rambling apology which completely baffled Valerie. Dad, with eyes still averted and a faint smile, said softly and cryptically, "Seattle *is* far away."

Then Valerie did the unspeakable in front of the partisan mob in Dad's room: she said something that made sense, and she called Dad by his first name. "Well, Kevin, it's not like we can just jump on the subway and get here any time we feel like it."

Margaret Mary, standing at the head of Dad's bed, aspirated audibly, clenched her jaws and fists and tightened her lips before turning toward the wall. Lucky for Margaret Mary we were at Georgetown University Hospital—just in case. Brendan, to his credit, as a husband and as a friend, said nothing to temper his wife's comment although he was tempted, and in time the conversation shifted to lighter matters such as global warming, embryonic stem cell research, and the immigration problem in the U.S. with no offense intended for Valerie of course.

When visiting hours were over, Brendan and Valerie filed out of Dad's room still carrying the undernourished plant they had picked up in the hospital gift shop. Earlier arrivals had long before trumped them and filled the room with bouquets upon bouquets of freshly cut flowers, Get Well balloons as big as pillows, and small hearty houseplants—African violets mostly. Brendan pulled me aside. There was desperation in his eyes. He was no longer the ace prosecuting attorney of Pierce County Washington. All that healing by a loving wife and intense therapy seemed to be evaporating. It was as if he had again become my nine-year-old baby brother right before me. There were honest-to-goodness tears of exasperation in his eyes.

"'*That's OK, Brendan.*' Did you hear him? '*That's OK, Brendan.*' Just what in the hell is that supposed to mean? Valerie and I come three thousand miles to be with him, and it's like we're crashing a private party or barging in on some secret society. All conversation stops. He doesn't look either one of us in the eye and merely says with that sad little smile of his, 'That's OK, Brendan.' *That's OK!? That's OK?* Just what in the hell does that mean? But then we all know perfectly well what it means, don't we? *Nice try but you came up a little short, again. I know that you could have done better, but I'll let it go, this time.* I can't deal with this again,

Michael. We cross the continent to be with him, and he still makes me feel guilty. Valerie? Thank God, she's impervious to all this crap. I hope you realize we can't keep running back to D.C. like this."

The only advice I could give him was, "Talk to your therapist and pray."

Valerie, meanwhile, was in the corner trying to strike up a conversation with Mary Margaret who kept her focus on the elaborate pattern of floor tiles and responded to Valerie's questions with edgy yes-or-no answers about her chemistry course at Holy Cross Academy. After a few minutes of that, Valerie shrugged, signed off from Mary Margaret, and worked her *iPhone,* scoping out deals on less expensive hotel rooms in D.C. just in case she and Brendan had to stay longer.

They didn't. Dad made a remarkable turn-around and was to be discharged soon so we could all "go back home. False alarm, everyone. Oh, and sorry, Valerie, for having to drag you all this way just to see a beat-up old man."

AARRGGHH!!!

The second summons to Georgetown University Hospital found Dad ashen but anointed and communicative while Brendan was stuck in Seattle preparing closing arguments for his first capital murder case.

On the second night of the second vigil, my father proceeded to recite a painstaking litany of all who had come to visit the previous night, a litany that would rival in length and complication a genealogy from Genesis, one that pointedly omitted Brendan and his wife Valerie. Mary Margaret noted the omission, and she and her mother Margaret Mary began to discuss again Valerie's "completely inappropriate comment to Dad" during their first visit as well as Brendan's current absence.

After Dad was released from Georgetown Hospital and returned home, I got a pivotal email from Brendan that said only, "I took your advice. It's working wonders. We're back on track. BK"

The third summons, a month later, found Dad sitting upright, his round, pink face beaming as we arrived on cue and out of breath. The priest on call for that occasion had already come and gone, and my father attributed his remarkable turnaround to the last rites which he said, "are better than any of this junk," as he made a sweeping gesture to the monitors, tubes, saline bags, boxes of tissue, water bottles, charts, all choking the room.

The last rites, officially called Anointing of the Sick, are to be administered judiciously, perhaps once or twice in a person's lifetime; however, my father managed to receive the sacrament almost as often as some people take vitamin supplements.

On the next night, Brendan arrived, but without Valerie.

Upon Brendan's arrival at the packed hospital room, Dad proceeded to report with encyclopedic accuracy the numbers and dispositions of last night's visitors as well as the visitors from earlier that day. I counted thirty-nine. Brendan would later report that, no, it was actually forty visitors. But whatever the number, the trap was baited. Brendan had not been among the privileged first-night visitors. Clearly, everyone knew the rules of the game: Brendan would of course have to stammer and apologize and be defensive and then feel guilty for doing his absolute best.

But something remarkable had happened to Brendan, what he had hinted at in his email. He was standing relaxed and confident. He was refusing to take the bait. He surveyed the hospital room packed like a subway at rush hour and countered with "Dad, I think it's absolutely wonderful that so many people care about you this much and come to visit you night after night. You're truly blessed."

My father lowered his eyes and pursed his lips almost imperceptibly, a sign of a momentary setback. Then my father deftly laid a series of in-law and who's-in-charge landmines for Brendan. "Please thank Valerie for letting you come and see me."

Letting you come and see me! Masterful! Only a Zen Master of Guilt could have devised that gambit. Every one of us wanted to see how Brendan was going to handle *that* one. It seemed a little like Jesus being baited by the Pharisees about paying tribute to God or to Caesar: no obvious answer seemed right. If Brendan responded that it had been *his* choice, he would come across as defensive and unconvincing, maybe even a bit like an adolescent insisting that *he* was in charge of *his* household, that Brendan Kilgariff wore the pants in *his* family, that no one *let him* go anywhere, that *he and he alone* made those decisions. If, however, Brendan focused on the Valerie part of the statement and made an excuse for her absence citing her job, then Dad would have reached checkmate permitting him to conclude all with the unstoppable grandchildren gambit where he hoped Valerie's career "would not continue to be so demanding to prevent her from having children."

Brendan, however, was equal to the move immediately before him, *"Please thank Valerie for letting you come and see me."* He stood firm and answered with a broad smile, "I'll tell her you said so, Dad. Valerie and I see eye-to-eye on so many things. I'm really lucky."

It was like throwing holy water on demons! In my mind's eye, I pictured the funhouse mirror reflection of Margaret Mary and Mary Margaret and Dad wincing a bit in pain, steam rising from their curved, scaly backs.

Dad was not to be so easily checked, however. He had one final assault—the inheritance gambit—designed to nullify any and all temporary victories. It was the atomic bomb of guilt. "You know, Brendan, I want to leave you and Valerie something, but I'm just concerned you'll have trouble getting all the things you want back to Seattle."

All the things you want. It made Brendan and Valerie sound like greedy opportunists; in only for the goodies. *Back to Seattle.* Well, that was the old abandonment gambit again.

But oddly enough, Margaret Mary herself foiled Dad's move and interjected with no little urgency in her voice, "I know that you've had your eye on Dad's Waterford crystal and his Wedgewood china for years, Brendan. Do you still plan on taking all of that?"

"Actually, I never gave Dad's things a moment's thought, Margaret Mary. I don't know where you got that idea. They're nice, and I've even said so, but I don't have a preference. You select whatever you want first; pick out something for me, perhaps a picture of all of us with Ma? Anything. All the rest is yours and Michael's."

More holy water and more demons cowering in the crowded hospital room. Dad had nothing left. An exhausted old Guilt-Warrior with an empty quiver at the perimeter of the convent, the Chess Master of Guilt checkmated by his own youngest son. Dad studied Brendan carefully. There was a long pause before Dad finally said, "You're very much like your mother, Brendan."

I could see admiration and affection in Dad's eyes for his youngest, the black sheep who had strayed so far from home, who had broken everyone's heart, and who now reminded Dad of Katherine Gottschalk Kilgariff.

Then Brendan placed an envelope in Dad's hand.

"Valerie bought this round-trip ticket for you, Dad. It's open-- ended. We want you to come visit whenever you feel better. Come anytime and stay as long as you feel like, but I think it would be terrific if you could join us next February for the Chinese New Year. It will be the Year of the Tiger. There will plenty of firecrackers and drums to drive Nian and the other evil spirits away, but I'll make sure we also get our throats blessed on the feast of St. Blaise."

Margaret Mary and Mary Margaret were dumbfounded as if someone had just taken a sledgehammer to the Waterford.

Dad smiled again and looked Brendan straight in the eye and said simply, "Thank you. I love you, Brendan."

And I knew my "Irish" father, Dan Kilgraiff, meant it.

About the author:

Dan Sullivan is thrilled to be selected as one of the finalists in this year's competition. This publication marks the fourth appearance of his fiction in Scribes Valley's publications. Dan is retired from teaching English literature and composition at St. Mary's Ryken (SMR) High School in Leonardtown, Maryland, but he keeps involved with SMR's students by tutoring in the evenings and on weekends. Dan is married to Jamie, a florist and manager at Giant Foods. He has been blessed with generous and remarkable children--Laura and Mark, an outstanding step-daughter Ploy, and loving grandchildren--Kyleigh, Erika, and Gavin. He is blessed indeed.

PEEKABOO DREAMS
©2010 by Tonya Mitchell

The start of it all was the cigarette, the one Darla found nestled in a crack on the front porch step, a Salem Light she might never have noticed if it weren't for the coral-pink smudge on the end. She went on into the house with the groceries and knew there wasn't enough food in those bags to keep them going until Dwayne's next paycheck. She stood and looked out the window over the kitchen sink and knew there wasn't anybody she knew smoked Salems. For weeks that half-burned stick laid there in the crack watching her come and go, watching her leave for work and come back again, and that little stick had been laughing; watching her and laughing.

It burned her still how stupid she'd been, and her on the verge of telling Dwayne about the money.

Darla set a plateful of food in front of her husband and sat down across from him. Dwayne took his suppers late on the nights he closed the Carpet Palace, although why he insisted on hot, heavy meals in summer was beyond her. It was one of the things the Petty men insisted on—hot food twice a day on the dinner table. Air coming through the window hot and clammy like a blow dryer but Dwayne would have his meat and potatoes steaming on a plate. She wondered how many hot meals there would be when she was gone and there was nobody to cook and do the cleaning up after.

"Mmm-mmm," Dwayne said, his jaw working. "Ain't nobody

makes a pork chop good as you, baby."

The meat was bought cheap, a fatty cut that stretched the dollar and—on account of it being poker night—the truth. Dwayne was a particular eater and complained most evenings about Darla's meals, but on the nights he did his card playing, Darla could set shoe leather in front of him and Dwayne would smack his lips and lay the sugar on. He wouldn't complain about Darla's cooking those nights, not when he was in high spirits contemplating the good time he'd be having shortly. She figured by the time he met that little blonde afterwards at the Days Inn over in Crawford, Darla would be over the state line and Kentucky would be just an itty-bitty spec in the rearview, a shriveled-up nothing like her heart was now, ever since she'd found that half-burned coral-pink-tipped cigarette on the porch.

Darla could feel the sweat oiling the back of her legs where they rested against the kitchen chair. She lifted one buttock and then the other, wiping the moisture from her skin as the tangy odor of Dwayne's underarms hit her nose. "What time you getting home?" she asked.

"Late."

Darla snorted. "Early's more like it," she said. "Early morning."

He went still and looked at her, the old Dwayne now. He could cut her with a single word or glance freezing like that and her heart would flip-flop. Dwayne wasn't a man who felt the need to explain himself and so she'd learned to bite her tongue. He had never hit her, not ever, but there were worst things a man could do.

Dwayne cleared his throat and when Darla looked at him again his face had shifted to something soft and agreeable. He gave her the wink that went with the smile, and the lie that came after was so easily told it might have been the truth if Darla hadn't known better. "I'll miss you, honey. You know that."

She shouldn't want him but she did. She shouldn't feel that bloom of lust between her legs, not with his cheating ways and her bags packed and ready. It was his eyes what did it; hazel they were, mostly brown with green near the centers. They reminded Darla of pasture, of untended fields. She liked how tall and lean he was, liked the way his dark hair took to curling when it got too long which it hardly ever did because he kept it short and neat. She even liked that chipped front tooth of his—that little missing notch that somehow still, after two years of marriage, made her go damp under the arms. She wanted him, even when he'd brought that little blonde into their house when Darla was at work.

Even when she knew he was just waiting, watching and waiting for her to bring up the money.

It had been months since he'd touched her, now he was getting what he wanted elsewhere, but she couldn't help remembering what it had been like before they were married. He'd wanted her all the time, ever since he'd first seen her dance up at the Peekaboo. In those days she'd left her self-respect at the door of that gentlemen's club and gyrated around a pole because it was the only work in Lewis County, Kentucky that grew a bank account big enough to start her a four-year liberal arts education. Five nights a week she'd twirled around that stage and fixed her gaze toward the back where the restrooms were, where the LADIES sign glowed red and reminded her of what she was—or wasn't. She'd hated the smoke and the caterwauling and the grabbing, but men itching for a night out without their wives paid good money to watch a pretty girl take her clothes off and if that was the price to get herself out of the blink-and-you-miss-it town of Sitwell, it had surely been worth it.

Mama always said you shouldn't count your chickens, but Darla had counted hers in the form of dollar bills for four years dancing at the Peekaboo, counted and danced and watched that savings build up. Then, when that account was fat enough, she'd planned to withdraw the money and get herself a degree. That nest egg was her one-way ticket out of Sitwell, to freedom, a whole new life. She wasn't like Mama, hunkered down and festering in Sitwell all these years, hoping the man who'd left her soon as she got pregnant would come back and meet his daughter one day. Darla was more like her Daddy who'd realized Sitwell was like a coat didn't fit anymore, something to get out of before it smothered and swallowed you whole.

So, she did her bit at the Peekaboo and let the customers think that gleam in her eye was for them, all for them. The tips were better that way. But it was her secret what glimmered, a dream that shined brighter, hotter than any light beaming down on that stage.

Then Dwayne had come along, new to Sitwell and the talk of every girl in town because he drove a fancy car and threw money around. She noticed him the first night he came into the Peekaboo, a tallish stranger in cowboy boots leaning against the wall in back who gave her a wink and a grin when she left the stage and headed for the dressing room. He came in the next night and the night after, and each time she felt his eyes on her like a hand lingering. Then he sent that bouquet of flowers—a dozen long-stemmed red roses—to her dressing room with a card that said he sure would like the phone number of the prettiest girl in Lewis County.

Darla meant to hold out at first. Men like him—good-looking and restless—were only after one thing. She turned him down three times when he asked her to dinner but then the other girls at the club told her if she thought she was too good for Dwayne Petty, she could just give him *their* numbers and that was that. The next time he asked, she said yes.

Dwayne took her to the only decent restaurant Sitwell had to offer and in the glow of candlelight she told him she planned on getting herself out of Sitwell and going to college. He took her hand and kissed her wrist and said maybe she could just hold off a bit because he wanted the chance to change her mind. Well, there wasn't a single girl living wouldn't have fallen for that turn of phrase. It was like something out of the movies. And so she gave him what he wanted that very night and didn't think she'd hear from him again but did. The flowers kept on coming and then expensive dinners in Louisville and Lexington and later, to top it off, a proposal with Dwayne down on one knee begging her to change her name.

Darla couldn't say no, didn't want to, not when he pressed hard against her and kissed her like he did and said they were bound to each other and there wasn't a thing could break them apart. They were married by the Justice of the Peace with Mama standing proud and Darla believing a man who said he'd follow her anywhere would surely follow her to college.

It wasn't her fault she found those shoe boxes under the bed when he left for work one day. She'd only meant to tidy up, being a new wife and all. In five minutes of riffling through pay stubs and credit card statements and letters from lenders Darla had the lay of things: Dwayne Petty was broke—flat-out over-extended living-on-credit broke. His take-home at the Carpet Palace wasn't what he'd made it out to be and all those things she thought he owned— the fancy Mustang convertible, the big screen TV, the fishing and hunting equipment and even her diamond ring—were plastic-bought, not really his or hers or theirs at all.

And so, she kept quiet about her money, knowing full-well Dwayne would only burn through it and in the burning set fire to every dream she'd ever had.

When Dwayne came home shortly after she found the boxes and asked her what she made dancing, Darla lied and gave him a figure that barely covered her bills. He slid her a grin that as good as called her a liar but then he'd looked down at her second-hand clothes and out the window at the old Taurus she drove and his face changed. The greed in his eyes scooted over and made room for new-found respectability. No wife of his, Dwayne told her, was going to work at a strip club. He made her go and quit her job at the Peekaboo but Darla knew it had nothing to do with virtues or morals or decency, but pride. The teasing and snickering from his buddies about his wife wearing lingerie to work wasn't worth it, now he thought her wages were piss-poor. And so Darla took a job waitressing at the diner where the pay was lousy like the food and every cent she made went to bills that grew and multiplied because Dwayne could no more put a lid on his spending than Darla could own up to twelve-thousand dollars tucked away at the Savings and Loan.

Sometimes at night, lying curled away from Dwayne, she'd picture her money stacked in neat little rows at the bank and that heavy weighed-down feeling would press at her and she'd wonder if it was guilt she was feeling keeping that money a secret or the slow death of her own dreams.

And then the tide turned a few months back when Dwayne came home late, outlined black and slender against the glow of the porch light.

"Jesus, Dwayne," she said from the couch where she'd been laying in the dark and wondering where her husband might have got to. "Where the hell you been?"

He stood there leaning against the door jamb, right hand stretching and tightening, stretching and tightening. Right then she should've known.

"Out," he said. "I been out."

"I can see that," Darla said and wrinkled her nose. "You been drinking, too. I guess it never occurred to you we don't have the money for you to go out boozing."

"That so?"

"Yeah, that's so. In case you hadn't noticed, we're broke."

"Oh, I noticed," Dwayne said, stepping from the doorway. "I notice every day when you complain and tell me what we can't pay or can't buy or can't afford."

"It's buying everything you see got us in this situation," Darla said.

"We had an extra twelve grand laying around, we wouldn't be in this situation."

She went still on the couch and felt something dark and ugly coming on and realized the quiet filling up the room was the sound of a wound-down clock, the sound of time run out. Darla moved to get away but Dwayne was there—shoving and pawing and pressing and ripping. He didn't stop until he was through, even when she cried and begged him to.

Afterwards he rolled off her and fumbled with his belt, and she wondered how he'd found out about that bankroll when she'd been so careful getting that post office box, so careful about those bank statements going to it and never, never, the house. And then not long after she'd found that cigarette and put two and two together to make three—herself, Dwayne and that coral-pink lipstick blonde worked down at the bank.

The grease was beginning to harden around Darla's pork chop, a little oil slick right there in the middle of her plate. She could smell the outer workings of her body—the oil of her scalp, the sour-sweet tears of sweat rivering down her back. The odor of dead grass drifted through the window and mingled with the stink of meat fat and turnip greens and she felt sick all of a sudden. She couldn't eat, couldn't sleep or move without breaking a sweat of late. In this heat there was no keeping dry; every pore flowed, and with the flowing came the thirst she could not satisfy. She felt continuously tied to damp, drowning in moist, sticky air.

The scrape of Dwayne's chair against the linoleum reminded her of a car starting and the light-headed feeling passed. Her own car would be starting soon and then she'd be gone and when Dwayne left a minute later and the screen door banged shut behind him it was the sound of a fresh beginning. Like an egg cracking and bursting open, the start of a dewy-new life.

Darla left the dishes where they were and pulled her suitcase from the back of the closet. The letters were still inside, those twin guarantees welcoming her to that university in Cincinnati and declaring her eligible for financial aid. After all these months the look of her name inked on paper still sent a shot of joy clean through her and the scent of wood pulp coming off the letterhead was the smell of liberty, hard-earned from dancing around a pole.

Darla lugged the suitcase out the front door into haze so thick the world had a slowed-down feel, like everything was under water. Heat soaking her skin and pulling her down, but she was floating, rising. Twelve thousand dollars cash in her purse—withdrawn that afternoon when that blonde left the bank on her lunch break—was no weight at all, but a life preserver buoying her up, up, to the surface, to a place where she could think and breathe and dream again.

And the cigarette wedged snug in that crack on the porch looked on, biding time and knowing.

The restaurant was squat, faded and worn-out looking from the outside, but none of that mattered to Darla. By the time, hours later, she slipped off the Interstate to fill up her tank and saw it leaning against the gas station, she was so hungry her legs felt hollowed out, so thirsty it seemed her teeth were wearing socks. She parked and walked on in, passing an air conditioner that sounded angry, like a thousand bees were trapped inside and hollering to get out.

The waitress wasn't much older than Darla herself, with hair dyed an odd state of orange that wrestled with the purple-red of her uniform. She set a tall glass of ice water in front of Darla who snatched it up and drank it down without regard for manners or conversation. Then she scribbled down Darla's order and walked away.

Apart from a man sitting at the counter, there were no other customers. His back was to her, but the way his hair curled over his shirt collar reminded Darla of her husband and she felt a stoppage in her dried-up heart, a little seizing up, then he turned to get the waitress's attention and she saw it wasn't Dwayne at all. The nose and chin were wrong, not cut sharp like Dwayne's. When he pulled a wallet from his back jean pocket and threw bills onto the counter, Darla looked away. She'd always hated the way Dwayne folded up cash in his own wallet—layered precise, so when he peeled off bills to pay for beer at the Speedy Mart or gas at the BP that same hundred-dollar bill was always on top. There for all the world to see like he was a man rolling in green and not somebody stretched so thin they had to live on boxed macaroni and cheese for days at a time until one of them got paid.

"I don't understand why you don't just break that hundred,"

she'd said.

"I ain't never going to break it," Dwayne had told her. "It's my lucky hundred."

Darla sniffed and felt the burning sand in her eye that was tears. It irked her how recollections of Dwayne tumbled out of her without cause, how scenes unraveled without proper go-ahead. Like thread from a runaway spool. Fact, it seemed her time with Dwayne had been one continuous line of lies and hurt that stretched unbroken far as the heart could feel.

"There anything else I can get you?" the waitress said.

Darla blinked and stowed the thought, then met the waitress's eyes. That's when she noticed, under the flaming fringe of those bangs, the girl's eyelids. They were painted a shimmery gray-white. The color of dirt on snow. Raw oyster. A fish's underbelly. Darla swallowed and felt her mouth water as a queasiness churned through her. The smell of grease and ketchup and pickle hit her nose and the floor started to shift.

She stood up and retched, the sickness coming out of her so sudden she could only stare down at it, numb and confused and shaking.

The waitress didn't move. Instead, her eyes took a walk over Darla's face, traveled down her arms to where Darla held her purse to her middle, and then came to rest on Darla's wedding band. Her lips moved then, the waitress's, but Darla couldn't make out the words. Her head was filled with a strange buzzing and she wondered if one of those bees had gotten loose from that air conditioner and found a way inside her head.

She stared at the scratching, those prickly capitals on the walls that ran and formed and formed again through the run-off of her tears. *MARTY CAN STICK IT WHERE THE SUN DON'T SHINE* and *FOR A GOOD TIME CALL YOUR MOTHER*. The waitress's words cut her deep again, those words Darla thought she hadn't heard as she'd stood there looking down at the mess she'd made on the restaurant floor.

I was sick just like that when I had my first.

Darla shifted her weight and squinted down at the little white stick, that other one having a good joke on her. She wondered how many of the girls who'd squatted here had waited for a pink line to form on such a stick, how many had sat and peed and read and contemplated their future—or the lack of it—in the dim light of that dirty restroom stuck on the back of the gas station. *For shame,* Mama would have said and the words suited those angry, sentence-stained walls and that cracked, rusted-out sink much as they did the turn her life might just be taking—depending. She did the math but couldn't remember when she'd had her last period. Dwayne hadn't been after her like he usually was—not now he had that pretty blonde to satisfy his needs. Darla had run out of pills but hadn't bothered to get more, not with so much on her mind. Not with Dwayne getting what he wanted somewhere else.

A flash of Dwayne in the doorway, hand working at his side, made her go still. Perched on that toilet seat, Darla felt again Dwayne's boiled-over rage at learning his wife had squirreled away twelve-grand worth of spending potential. She smelled once more Dwayne's foul, bourbon-marinated breath as he'd panted over her, having his way. She knew then, knew for sure, that was the night what did it, got her in a family way. And when that little white, pink-tipped stick in her hand proved it three minutes later she felt something wither inside her and something else bloom.

Far as she was concerned, there was only one thing you could give and keep at the same time and that was your word and she gave it, her word, to her baby right then and there. *I'll hold on to you. I'll protect you and love you just like my mama done me.* Mama, who'd stood firm all those years ago and watched her belly grow fast and bold as the talk in town, talk about a skirt-chasing husband who'd left his angel wife. Darla wasn't like her daddy who'd spent most nights down the bar telling anybody who'd listen marriage wasn't a word but a sentence and he was about done serving his. Even Dwayne, with his wandering eye and two-timing heart, wouldn't leave. He might go away a night or two like all the

Petty men had a way of doing when they were chasing tail, but he'd come back. He always came back.

Dwayne wouldn't ever know, not ever. If she drove straight-through, she'd be home before he left the Days Inn with that blonde in the morning. Tomorrow she'd buy a nice nursery, the best her money could buy and then put the rest in a college fund for baby before Dwayne could say boo about it. Soon enough it wouldn't be that blonde keeping him up nights, but a squalling baby needed a feeding.

When she stepped out into the harsh fluorescents of the parking lot, Darla felt her dried-up raisin heart blossom for want of a baby girl with eyes the color of untended pastures and the little white stick caught in that crack in the tile was already fading, quick as the memory of wood pulp that had once smelled of liberty.

About the author:

Tonya Mitchell received her BA in journalism from Indiana University. For many years she worked in marketing in the food and toy industries but the love of writing never left her. For the last three years she has taken a more serious approach to writing, dedicating her time at the keyboard whenever time allows. She is the recipient of the Best of Ohio Writer award in short fiction and her historical non-fiction is forthcoming in *The Copperfield Review*. "Peekabo Dreams" is her third published story. She lives with her husband and three boys in Cincinnati, Ohio and is currently at work on a novel.

MOON ROCKS
©2010 by Michelle Wotowiec

The restaurant lights were dim, giving the illusion of romance. A fifty-five-year-old woman confidently strutted to the table in the corner. There, she found Romance waiting at the table, waiting for her to sit down, cross her legs, and bat her eyelashes. Romance was in the form of a blonde-haired gentleman with perfect teeth and tanned skin, who happened to think she was the most beautiful woman he had ever laid his eyes on. After the perfect dinner (*Have you tried our crab cakes? They are a perfect complement to our Reisling*), he would look her in the eyes and promise her true happiness for the rest of her life. And true happiness, she would later reminisce, had been found at Sparkle Eats, the national chain employing ambitious single mothers, drug addicts, and poor college students.

I was young the first time I had sex. Very young. *Too* young. The sixteen-year-old kid's name was not Romance. He had fire red hair and a voice that sank ships. *My* ship. I met him at a skating rink and we spent hours skating around in circles, I backward and he forward, telling each other anything we thought might spark interest in the other. I don't know what color his eyes were, or even his mother's first name. I spent ten months with him in the skating rink eating fried cheese sticks and cheap pizza, in my parents' basement on an old mattress on the floor, and out next to a large maple tree lying on a sheet he would bring with him in his

Adidas backpack. Not once did he take me to dinner and not once did I have the self-respect to expect it.

The sixty-year-old woman with abnormally defined cheekbones had a tiny nose and slid into the restaurant like a slug. I wondered if she had been teased growing up. She had never been beautiful. Did she come into this restaurant because of the dim lights? Did she believe in the false promise, this idea of a true happiness waiting to be found in the shadows?

Where is beauty? Was this woman beautiful? She was far from a blonde-haired bombshell. Her body had no concrete shape and her skin fell onto her body in flaps. Flap of skin on top of flap of skin. In the dim dinner lighting, this woman melted into the walls of the restaurant. No one will take a second glance at her, except me. I am the server. I am her background which she will take little to no notice of. She will treat me the way the world treats her, she will use me for what she wants. I am nothing more than a stepping stone in getting her crab cakes and devouring the empty promise they hold.

The man accompanying her was in his forties, with yellow teeth, and had bulging veins on the sides of his upper forehead. I imagined him at home reading the newspaper with his right elbow bent on top of a small cedar table, his hand cradling his chin and his temples throbbing as she slugged around the small house with powder blue walls.

I grew up pretty. Pretty enough to get attention I didn't need. I never slugged around and met unattractive men in restaurants. I wore tight tank tops and short shorts while boys whispered promises in my ears. The same promises the slug lady wanted to hear. I wish I had the nerve to tell her those promises are never real. At least they weren't for me. Every slippery-tongued boy left me high and dry, wrapped up in a dirty bed sheet. Looking back at it now, I would have rather hidden in the shadows of a restaurant, eating crab cakes with the hopes of something better than stare at the ceiling as I heard the door slam behind them.

I walked over to the table to introduce myself to the slug woman and her companion. When I approached the table she didn't allow me time to say my name, or even hello. She granted me nothing more than a dry, snooty "Water with lemon. He'll take a coffee—" she cleared her throat and made direct eye contact with me while I fiddled to find my pad of paper and pen, "A *fresh* coffee." She looked at me but saw nothing more than just another waitress. She could have been talking to Obama dressed in a black uniform with an apron tied around his waist. Or Madonna. Or even Jesus for all she knew.

I smiled and replied, "Of course, our coffee is always fresh."

During the winter of 2006, I woke up to my alarm at seven a.m. every morning. It was an upbeat jingle provided by Verizon which I had come to hear in my dreams. Every morning I walked with cement feet up the stairs and scurried into the kitchen. I dumped out the old coffee, filled the coffee maker with fresh water, and put in three scoops of Folgers Dark Roast. As it brewed, I sat at the kitchen island with my head in the palms of my hands as I waited to hear Dad open his bedroom door and come down the stairs.

We spent twenty minutes together, talking about anything and everything. He would tell me about the guys who worked for him in his mechanic shop. The one guy, Pokey, put butterfly stickers all over the dashboard of his car. Fred, the nineteen-year-old kid, was going to be a dad within the next three weeks. Scott Jr. just got out of prison after serving a seven-year sentence for raping his nine-year-old nephew.

I would tell him about school and the professors I liked, and about the long drive to Kent State University, and the weird people I met along the way in gas stations and in the lines of Subway.

The cranky couple ate their greasy burgers, left a ten percent tip, and went home to their imaginary white house with blue trim.

As I was wiping down the germs, crumbs, and tiny pools of saliva left behind on the table, I overheard two women talking a few tables away:

"Oh, I *know*. She definitely brought that on herself. What was she thinking, telling him all that stuff about her childhood?" Her voice was squeaky like a mouse. "Stuff like that is better left unsaid. We just don't *talk* about those things. Lord knows why she didn't know any better."

Her face looked white, ghostlike under the light hanging above her head. I imagined she was a reaper who was placing some sort of universal code on what is proper female etiquette, and the *Do*s and *Don't*s of Romance. Then I saw myself punching her in the face and screaming, "W*e are people, not puppets!*" She would look at me dumbfounded, terror stricken, and in a shaky voice would respond, "But we are *women!*"

"That's exactly what I said. She should have just kept it all a secret and he would still be *with* her. He would have never treated her that way in a million years had he not known...."

This woman's voice was much deeper. Unlike her gossipy friend, she was not sitting directly below the light so her skin looked darker—almost Indian—and I imagined her to be a character from *Slumdog Millionaire*. I then realized how uninformed I am on unfamiliar races and there is no way that everyone with a dark complexion comes from the slums of India.

"I mean," her voice grew quieter, "you *know* he wouldn't have laid a hand on her had the circumstances been different."

"So anyway, not to change the subject, but I have been *dying* to ask you," Mousey continued, "is it true about Gerry? Did he really cheat on you?"

Slum Lady didn't respond as she scooped her hair behind her ears and cupped her head in her hands.

I was six and Lisa was eight the night my mother's affair became public. The rain was falling like bowling balls off of the old barn roof and the thunder sounded like my grandfather when he cleared his throat before he spoke. My father didn't know my mother had left the house that night. Lisa, my father, and I had all fallen asleep in the living room watching *Dolls* when I heard the phone ringing and Dad stumbling toward it in slow motion.

"H-Hello?" His voice was scratchy and far away. My toes felt cold as I recovered them under the dark blue comforter.

"W-What? How?" A few long seconds passed. "Where? Who?" He was silent again. At six years old I was able to feel his pain and fear as he breathed in deeply from a room away. "I'm going to have to take the girls with me. I can't leave them here. We'll be there as soon as we can."

Lisa nudged my leg with hers and looked me in the eye. She looked afraid as Dad walked back into the living room.

"There has been an accident, girls. We need to leave right away. Mommy is hurt really bad." Tears streamed down his cheeks as he helped us off the couch and into our coats.

It was the first time I saw my father cry. I later found out the true story and what had actually happened that night. She was on her way home from Jim's house and had fallen asleep at the wheel. Jim was a nineteen-year-old bartender who apparently thought my mother was very pretty. At least until her face was ripped off her skull in the accident that night.

I noticed my hand wasn't moving. I was standing against the half-cleaned table like a stuffed cat. I continued wiping areas I had probably already gotten too when I saw the hostess seat another table. I needed to greet them. Greet. Smile. Smile. Greet. Greet. Greet. Smile. It was all so repetitive. I was never like this before. I never looked at someone and imagined how cheap they were going to be with leaving the tip. Or how generous. I never cringed at the site of old people or people of foreign nationalities. I never knew what bad tippers they were.

Who was I? What choices had gotten me to that exact spot at that exact moment feeling that exact way? The speakers around me played a song about love. Generic love. How great love makes you feel and how lucky you are to have it. The love we are told to find and how we should feel about it. The love I never felt and would never find.

Six months after my mother's accident, a boy kissed me for the first time. His name was Travis and he had bright, slimy, red lips and blonde hair. He was my friend. We would play together on the living room floor while my mother sat in a Lazy Boy, peering through her gauzed mask wrapped around her face like a mummy.

One night I woke up and he was sitting next to me smiling, showing me his tiny fingers. "I was touching your crotch. I had my fingers inside." He looked right at me when he said it, smiling. I knew it was wrong. Something about him doing that was wrong.

If it were today, I would have cried, I think. Maybe I would have screamed. Or kicked. Anything but turn onto my side, face the wall, and pretend to go back to sleep like I did that night with Travis. He didn't know I spent the rest of that night with my eyes open and my stomach in my throat.

"Hi, welcome to Sparkle Eats. How are you?" It was a young couple; both men had dark hair and wore blue jeans.

These guys were going to be talkative, and seeing as we weren't busy, I was almost relieved to have a conversation with someone besides myself. They told me they were planning on going to see some Brad Pitt movie tonight but the snow kept them in. By the time the snow let up, they figured they might as well salvage what they could of the night and grab a bite to eat. They sat in the cold car bickering about which restaurant had the best burgers in town. Mike's Grill came in a close second, but they were here sitting at my table so I knew who the winner was.

As the man on the right continued to tell me about the car problems he had encountered this week, I thought about what my grandmother would think of him. What the majority of the world thinks about him. He isn't a man, many would say, because he is romantically involved with another man. What does something like that take away from his character? If he was interested in a woman, would my grandmother think that he would be telling me about some other type of car problem? Or maybe he would be telling me about baseball or some hot new babe on *Desperate Housewives*?

I was eleven years old, sitting in the back seat of my mother's fire red Cougar next to my best friend. We were parked in our driveway. Thinking back, I have no idea what we were doing sitting in the car with our seatbelts on when the car had no destination. There was no one in the driver's seat; it was only me and my friend. Let's pretend we had just gotten home from something amazing. Like a circus. An animal-friendly circus. It was nice outside and the windows were down. I could hear two birds singing back and forth from the large maple tree to my right. I imagined they were proclaiming their love for one another through song, the way it should be proclaimed. My friend's hair was a light brown. Her eyes were green. She didn't talk much. In fact, I don't think she really talked at all. We were friends because our moms were friends and it was easier for them to have us play together than have to worry about finding two different sitters.

My friend was looking at my hands. At my short stubby fingers.

"What?" I was irritated and self-conscious.

"Want to play a game?" One of the few times she actually spoke. I didn't see anything strange in having a best friend who I had never really talked to. She held her hand out so I could see it.

"Okay, I guess."

"Stick out your tongue and close your eyes."

I looked at her for five long seconds before I finally submitted. I remember realizing how small I was when my eyes closed. I was, for the first time, aware of my legs dangling and my feet floating in the air. The seatbelt was tight around my tiny waist and I had an urge to pull it off. It took blocking off one sense to feel another. I was young. I suddenly felt as if I didn't quite fit in that car, in my body. I didn't fit. I didn't know this feeling would stick with me for the rest of my life.

Then I felt her moist, warm tongue against mine and my eyes involuntarily opened. I didn't want them to open. I had never seen her so close. I had never seen anyone so close. I saw the skin of her cheeks and the freckles lining her nose. I didn't know the feeling. I wasn't ready for the feeling. Was it love? Was that what love is or what love means?

The car door swung open and my mom was screaming, tightly squeezing my boney arm that didn't fit me and fighting with the seatbelt that wanted me to stay there in the car with my friend.

"Don't you ever! Don't you even *think* about it!"

I wasn't sure if my mother was screaming at me or at my friend as she fought my seatbelt buckle and ripped me out of the car.

As I cleared the plates off the table left behind by the two men, I suddenly felt so tired of cleaning. Cleaning up after myself, cleaning up after other people, cleaning in general. I was a robot. I couldn't think of one day that had passed that I had not cleaned *something*. I imagined what the restaurant would look like if I decided to stop cleaning it. If I refused to clean the tables, would people still sit in them to eat? What is more important, eating or sitting at a clean table? In my fantasy world, I saw the restaurant full of greasy couples eating greasy burgers from stacks of dirty plates, surrounded by dirty napkins and mountains of Pepsi glasses and lobster tail shells.

On Fridays I cleaned my parents' house. Every Friday for a very long time. Mom worked long hard hours and told me I was a good daughter and kissed my forehead when I helped her out. And she paid me. Not much, but enough for me to continue being a good daughter.

I had this white cleaning bucket that she had given me to fill with water so I could scrub the white tiled countertops and the crevices between the deep fryer and the wall.

I say *had* because I am about to tell you a terrible story that will twist your stomach and you will probably think about it every time you see a white cleaning bucket, a bottle of Pine-Sol, or a dead cat.

Poessy—this tiger-striped tabby cat that had lived with us for a few years. Years I spent stoned, too stoned to remember to dump the bucket of Pine-Sol water. Mom continuously reminded me to take it outside and dump it. Mom, the crazy Mom who cheated on my father and had her face reconstructed, *she* remembered to tell me to dump the water. I didn't. I kept forgetting. I was stoned, literally, all the time.

On a Friday night, Poessy decided to drink from the bucket. Did she not smell the Pine-Sol? Did she forget that she had a full water dish in the mudroom? Was she trying to punish me for, well, for everything? I wish I could find her now, her cat soul, and ask her why she waited five days to drink from the bucket. I would tell her that almost ten years later, I haven't forgotten about her and I haven't been able to forgive myself.

I was stoned when I found her sprawled out on the counter next to the bucket. She was lying on the white-tiled counter, belly up and legs stretched in a way that seemed to defy physics. She wasn't supposed to be on the counter. She knew better. The sound her body made as it hit the floor reminded me of the sound of wet Play-Doh hitting a cement floor.

When she didn't land on her feet, I realized she was hurt. Or sick. There was a large puddle of vomit where she was lying on the counter. I was so stoned and I wanted to be anywhere but in that kitchen right then, but when I picked up her body of clay, her eyes were open. She was crying a way that no creature should ever cry and her body was limp and yet it was clay and she just kept crying and I was so stoned and....

The pretty blonde host sat Joe and Stan, my regulars, at table thirty-five. They are brothers in their fifties who spend one night a week together catching up on their old-man lives over steaks or crab cakes.

I always feel a sense of relief when they come in and always a weird sense of regret when they walk out. I should be lucky enough to leave the restaurant and not have to come back for an entire week.

"Hey, Joe, Stan. What are we having tonight? A *Blue Moon* and *Sam Summer*?" I feel as if I am in a Lifetime movie and I am the washed-up waitress who memorizes customer's orders. Her feet are stuck in cement and she continues to dream of a better life. I'm only twenty-three. I can't be washed up yet, can I? There's more. There has got to be more.

"Hey, sweetheart. Yes, that sounds great." Joe is about six feet tall and very slender. He wears large glasses that sit nicely on the bridge of his elongated nose.

"Yes, good to see you. I'll take that *Blue Moon*. The beer of the astronauts." Stan smiled goofily as he did every time he gave me the exact same line. I always waited for him to tell me that he wanted to travel through space, or maybe that he had an old childhood dream of being an astronaut.

There is a First Merit Bank where a playground was when I was a kid. It wasn't a particularly special or impressive playground, but it was where all the kids in town flocked after school every day. Next to the rusty swing set and not-so-safe teeter totters, there was an old silver and white slide shaped like a rocket. My rocket slide. Dad used to tell me that it would eventually launch to the moon. The blue moon and my rocket slide appeared to have a destiny.

"What do you mean it will launch to the moon, Dad? Where is the engine?"

"It doesn't need an engine, sweetheart. Just look at it, it *is* a rocket. It is bound to launch. Go enjoy it while you can!" His skin was young then, the skin of a man in his late twenties. Skin that hid all of Mom's secrets and encased all of the pain those secrets caused him.

Sometimes I played along with him, in fear his feelings would be hurt if he knew I saw through his fib.

Five years later, I would be one of the kids with the Sharpie, writing profanities on the sides of the slide. Dad didn't foresee me having my first French kiss at the top of the rocket slide. It was with a boy who had light brown freckles and large moist lips and a joint cupped behind his ear. It was this same boy who would introduce me to almost everything a father wouldn't want their daughter introduced to. A launching of sorts, I suppose.

That rocket slide should have gone to the moon and I should have gone with it.

Have you ever felt trapped?

Trapped. Cliché? Maybe. I don't know when the feeling first crept up, if maybe it *was* that day in the car when I closed my eyes and felt my best friend's tongue against mine. Or if maybe it isn't an original feeling. Maybe I watched one too many dramatic movies where this feeling was reinforced through beautiful crying women with mascara running down their cheeks. Maybe I watched one too many Disney movies and got tired of waiting for my ridiculously happy ending.

Sometimes when I am here, in this restaurant, scrubbing down the same tables or greeting the same faceless, meaningless people, over and over and over and over—I feel inside myself. Like my body is suffocating me or holding me back. Too inside. Lonely. And then I have this urge to flee. To just run. It wouldn't even matter where I ran to. Even if I simply ran around the restaurant as fast as I could, my arms flailing, screaming at the top of my lungs, maybe I might feel better. Best case scenario, I could run out the door, into the frozen tundra, throw off my shoes one-by-one while in my sprinting frenzy and make my way across the world barefoot. If the world is to be crossed, it needs to be crossed with bare feet.

As I pushed the Bissel around the floor, I wondered what Stan or Joe might say if I told them any of this. Would they think I was crazy? Or maybe joking? Would they still tell me lighthearted jokes and believe me when I laughed at them?

The next thing I knew, I was walking toward them

involuntarily. I looked straight at Stan and said, "I want to cross the world barefoot."

"Barefoot?"

Stan's reaction surprised me. Before I even realized I was telling them my fantasy, I felt ashamed and embarrassed.

He placed his elbows on the table and clasped his hands. "Well, I think I might just agree with you, young lady."

The summer of 1987, I was eleven and my sister thirteen. It was mid-July and I had begged my sister to take me with her to her friend's farm. I was young and needy and my sister hated me for it. I didn't want to stay in the living room in front of the television, envisioning all the fun Lisa was having without me.

Lisa's hair was curly and brown and her face was the most flawless and beautiful face I had ever seen. I imagined her as a runway model with bouncy hair, wearing flashy colors. Jericka, her foreign friend from I-still-don't-know-where, had decided we would go for a walk down the newly paved country road. It was open land. Just like in those movies you have seen. There was nothing but open fields spotted with cows and horses and lined with large maple trees. I loved it. I belonged in those open fields.

Beads of sweat ran from my armpits and down my sides. I remember the way the salty sweat burned as it dripped down my forehead, slipped past my eyelashes, and fell into my eyes. I had forgotten my sequined blue flip flops on Jericka's porch. The asphalt felt like hot coals under my feet. I tiptoed and hopped as long as I could before I cried and begged them to slow down, but they continued walking and laughing and walking, ignoring the pleas of the annoying little sister. I finally turned around and walked through the ditch, dodging old cigarette butts, shards of broken glass, and decaying animal carcasses until I reached her porch. I sat next to her white Shepherd named Max and waited for them to return. I spent hours picking at the sticky tar and bloody blisters.

* * *

"It was good seeing you, as always!" Stan and Joe say in unison as they get out of their booth and walk to the door.

"You, too. I'll see you guys soon." I smile as I carry dirty dishes past them and back into the kitchen.

After they leave, I put the fifteen-dollar tip they left me into my pocket. I immediately wonder if I am really worth fifteen dollars. If walking back and forth to the kitchen, taking the order, bringing out the food, and cleaning up the mess is really worth fifteen dollars.

What is fifteen dollars, anyway? Three bags of tortellini. A little less than three packs of cigarettes. A cheap pair of shoes from Wal-Mart. A pair of jeans off the clearance rack.

"Do you really need *that* shirt, sweetheart? It is sixty-five dollars. That is a *lot* of money for a piece of fabric." Mom was thin. Very thin. Maybe *too* thin. Her cheek bones seemed to start at her forehead.

"Fine. Whatever, Mom." I was young. So young. A naïve twelve-year-old who wanted to be pretty and popular. I turned and looked away from her, pretending to get ready to leave the store.

"Don't be mad, Jelly Bean. We can get it. Just this once." She was smiling. Her mouth was lined in new wrinkles. Crow's feet of the mouth. She was too young to have wrinkles on her face and if I had been any older, or maybe considerate, I would have seen that she didn't have the money to spend on the things I thought I needed, or the heart to disappoint me.

Later that night I sat on the steps behind the kitchen wearing my new shirt, clipping my bright pink toe nails. I overheard Mom crying in the kitchen, the same kitchen where Dad answered that fateful phone call years earlier. Dad was telling her how much money they didn't have and how she was running them to the ground.

"You don't know how it is, John! You just don't understand! Try raising these two girls all alone like I do." Her voice was scratchy and sad.

"You're not alone. I am right here!" Dad sounded frustrated with her as I heard her walk into the dining room.

I was fifteen when I realized the annoying phone calls were bill collectors who were hounding my mother for the forty thousand dollars she didn't have. I was eighteen before I realized a lot of the money she owed was spent on me.

An old man wearing a blue baseball cap, and a younger woman in a bright red coat come into the restaurant and sit at table thirty-seven. There is no feeling of romance or of a hope for something better.

"Hi, how are you tonight?" I feel small and unimportant next to this woman with her tight blonde curls and pressed suit.

"Fine, thanks."

"Good. Can I start you with something to drink?"

"Sure."

"We offer Coke products: Coke, Diet Coke, Root Beer, Dr. Pepper, Sprite, Minute Maid Lemonade, and Strawberry Tea. We are featuring four-dollar Tennessee Teas and three-dollar Sangrias: red, white, and blackberry."

"I'll take a Diet, please. Dad, do you want a coffee?" Her flawlessly applied pink lipstick accents her bright white teeth.

"Yeah, that's fine." His voice is rough, as if he has gravel stuck deep in his throat. It is obvious he really cares what he has to drink. I feel a sort of pity for him, whatever kind of pity a twenty-something-year-old has the right to feel for a seventy-year-old man.

I watch him look to his right and place his hand lightly on his thigh. His pants look old and worn. Suddenly I am aware that he doesn't want to be here. It couldn't be more obvious and I wish I could tell this lady to take him home. "He doesn't want to be here, can't you see?" I imagine telling her. Her flawless pink lips would tighten and she would clear her throat, "Excuse me, what did you just say?" I would immediately coil and my heart would race. I would regret ever saying anything to her about it, knowing I would never have the nerve to help the man on my own terms. Some people you just can't get through to, and she is probably one of them.

Instead, I grabbed the Diet Coke and the coffee from the back and make my way back over to the table. I took a quick glance at a pamphlet as I placed the drinks onto the table. It appeared to be promoting some sort of group home a few cities away. The colors of the pamphlet were bright; red, yellow, light blue, and white. An eighty-year-old woman with a plastered smile appeared on the cover next to three or four children wearing long pony tails and loose fitting blue jeans. The sun was setting and in large print it read *Home is Here.*

The man hadn't opened his menu. His tissue paper skin was almost see-through. He continued to look out the window and I knew he was trying his best not to see the smiling old women and the ponytailed children.

"Would you like a minute to look over the menu or do you have any questions I can answer for you?"

"No, we're ready." She closed her menu with authority, the type of authority a child should never feel over her parent. "Dad, tell the lady what you would like for dinner." She tapped her hand on the tabletop. "Hey, Dad?"

He turned his head away from the window and stared at his lap. His eyes were red and moist and I tried not to look at him. No one wants to see an old man cry. There is something about tears falling down an elder's face that makes me feel like some universal law is being shattered. I need elders to be strong and I need them to be some sort of hope. I don't want my future to hold sitting in a booth at a restaurant with my child, being told I was being moved into a group home to die. I couldn't let my future hold that.

"Dad, if you're going to be like this, I'm just going to order food for you. I don't have all night to spend here and you know that. Kiley has choir practice and you know how important that is to her." She was growing noticeably more upset. She couldn't understand   why   her   father   wouldn't   care   about   his granddaughter's weekly choir practice.

The worst parts about being a server are moments like those: moments when two people are on an intimate level where so much history and so much pain are involved. I, the server, am cemented to the floor, standing awkwardly with a pen and paper in my hand. The fake smile on my face hides all of my own baggage while I try to remind myself how to block out theirs. I don't belong there. They don't belong there. It is like another dimension that normally reasonable people get sucked into and are forced to live moments of pure hell. Not one of the three of us wanted to be there in the restaurant that night.

"Okay, fine. I'm just going to order for him, then." She no longer talks to him but talks to me. She wants my sympathy. "We'll both be having the pasta with the grilled chicken and alfredo sauce. I'll take the salad bar and you can get him a bowl of chicken noodle soup to start." She looked at my forehead and I felt myself shrink. I wanted to switch positions with her. I wanted to tell her to fuck off and give her father a minute to decide what he wanted to eat.

"Okay, sounds good. I'll send that through for you," I robotically responded as I embraced the tight feeling in my stomach. The pain I felt reminded me I would never take my father to a restaurant with a group home pamphlet. I would never be like her.

Summer 2003. I sat Indian-style on the grass in a black tank top and jean shorts that were too short. I was seventeen. I don't remember what inspired me to stop and sit in the grass, or if it was even about being inspired. Maybe I just robotically decided to sit. It doesn't matter. For fifteen long seconds, I felt grateful. I felt as if I was sitting on top of my skin. I looked up at the clouds and it was one of the few times in my life when I felt nothing but true happiness. I wish I could give you some sort of uplifting story on how I came to find a good character within myself or how maybe I apologized to my mother for the financial stress I repeatedly gave her. I wish I could tell you that I confronted the boy with blonde hair and bright red lips. Or that Poessy woke up and told me she was playing a practical joke on me, that she didn't really drink out of that bucket of Pine-Sol water. I want to tell you that my father forgave my mother for that rainy night or that my mother forgave herself.

But for those long fifteen seconds staring at the clouds, I felt alive. I felt so insignificant and yet so important. I felt real and I felt hope. I believed I could remind my parents that they loved each other, through everything, and that love was enough. I would send them into the restaurant to sit in the dimly lit booth and they would fall in love all over again over crab cakes and Reisling.

I walked back over to the table with refills in my hands. The woman had her legs crossed tightly, reading over the pamphlet and her father was staring at his lap.

"What do you have there?" I felt the sting of the question as it slipped through my lips involuntarily.

"Oh, this? This is a nice place we're thinking about sending my father." She began to open it but I turned my glance to her father. "Isn't that right, Dad?"

He began to sob. A hurricane came through this man's eyes as he let out all of his anger and pain. He let his entire life out onto the table through his tears. I wanted to help him. I wanted to offer to take care of him. I would move in with him and make sure he didn't forget to turn the stove off. I would make sure he didn't miss any appointments and remembered all of the grandchildren's birthdays.

"Oh, Dad—" She stood up and sat next to her father, hugging him tightly. "Dad, it's for the best. I promise you. I would never hurt you or do anything to make you upset, you know that."

"But I don't need to go. I'm fine."

"Ever since Mom died you have lived alone doing nothing but drinking hot tea and reading old newspapers. I just can't have that. This will be much better for you."

"It's a *hospital,* Maria. Not a home. I am not forgetful or weak. I am just fine. Please, I am begging you, don't make me go."

"Dad, you are old, too old to live on your own soon. You are becoming the wallpaper. I can't keep worrying about you. But you don't have to worry. I'll visit you all the time."

He continued to cry, tears rolling down his tissue-paper cheeks and onto his lap.

I felt even smaller. Miniscule. I was reminded that whether or not someone asked me how I was doing, whether they worried if I was listening or not, whether two old brothers had nothing to look forward to but dinner at this restaurant, or if my pockets were overflowing with rubies and moon rocks, it didn't really matter.

None of it mattered.

About the author:

Michelle Wotowiec was born in Spencer, Ohio and graduated from Black River High School in 2004. She received her bachelor degree in English with a minor in writing from Kent State University in 2008. Michelle has been writing fiction and nonfiction for the past two years. She has also been a server for the past two years, playing a large part in her writing "Moon Rocks," which is her first piece to be accepted for publication.

GOING HOME ON LINEA-B
©2010 by Jean Tschohl Quinn

Buenos Aires was not working for her. Halfway through her internship, Marisol figured she wouldn't last till its end. The first month had slipped by in confusion over the accent. It was so different from her own parents' Watsonville Spanish; so *rapido* and shushy and sing-songy. She hadn't expected to lose another month trying to decipher the *porteño* colloquialisms. No one would explain them. They just laughed proudly about their own cleverness. More irritating was their proud bigotry against the indigenous. She was beautiful by most standards with high cheekbones, full lips and black hair; however, in BsAs she was just a *negrita* and was treated like anyone else that was not of European descent in a myriad of tiny passive-aggressive ways. Never mind that she was there working for her Master's degree and quite fluent in both international business Spanish and the *porteño* dialect by the end of her third month in town. She was *negrita* and, therefore, undeserving of respect.

It wasn't all bad. She enjoyed the café around the corner from the room she rented. The evening manager was friendly. They had pleasant conversations. He treated her respectfully. He would even explain the colloquialisms, if she could remember them exactly right; otherwise, he'd just shrug. Some days, her regular stop for *te con leche* was all that kept her from packing it in completely. The few times she went out with coworkers thus far had been less pleasant. She ended up being pawed and growled at as alcohol loosened the fingers and tongues of the men she met. No, Marisol would simply count down the days until the internship was over. That day, however, another ninety days, seemed impossible.

She left her office, her boots shuffling through the trash that floated down the street. The burgeoning recycling industry consisted of *cartoñeros* tearing through garbage receptacles in search of recyclable materials, leaving the remains to the mercy of roaming dogs and the weather.

She kept her head down to avoid the graffiti that desecrated all the vertical surfaces and concentrate on the dog crap that graced the horizontal. She stopped at the corner and sighed. The *Subte* home would take two transfers in congested stations. She did not want to take the bus again, not after what had happened that morning. Standing nose-to-nose with a middle-aged man for several minutes in the rush hour crush, she returned his wide smile. Up until that point, she had not seen a smile on a bus—on the street or the *Subte* either for that matter. She foolishly thought it was a gesture of friendliness. She wasn't sure if his pushing up against her was accidental, until he fondled her openly just as he turned to get off the bus. She called out, "How dare you!" The indignity and violation were met only with icy stares from the people around her. He winked at the bus driver as he stepped off. Someone tried to trip her as she got off at the next stop.

The day slid into early darkness without so much as a glimpse of a weak, winter sun breaking through to her tiny office window. A scruffy-looking youth shoved a flyer for a nearby restaurant into her hand. On the other side of the street, a man in a red jacket with a red fuzzy wig handed her a coupon for a new headache product. Just outside the *Subte* station at *Pichincha*, someone else handed her a third flyer for a live nude show—both sexes.

The wind eddied in the descending stairs causing hundreds of discarded *Subte* tickets to dance at her feet. She flowed with the rest of people through the turnstiles towards *Bolivar* and waited for the next train. The tile mural of the mountains had recently been defaced with copious amounts of uninteresting graffiti. She and several others entered the car.

A beggar, an indigenous-looking *joven* probably from Paraguay, walked through the car placing a holy card stapled to a small package of multicolored hair ties on the knees of each of the seated passengers, handing the packs to those who were standing if they hadn't managed a vague no-thank-you wave in time. Marisol pretended to study the *Subte* plan above the doors, then to read the flyers still in her hand. The beggar gathered up the unwanted wares and the few guilt-sodden pesos by the next stop.

Marisol switched lines at Independencia to Linea-C towards Retiro. She rode the next three stops in sardine-like peace and got off at the madness of the *9 de Julio* interchange, dropping into the river of people crossing to their respective *linea*s. Waiting silently, she listened to a loud, slightly out-of-tune singer accompanied by a brooding guitarist on the Linea-B platform. Of course, they were performing tangos, each describing wounds and heartbreaks that could depress Mickey Mouse. She tossed a 5-peso note into the open guitar case. The generosity raised a few eyebrows. Two young men moving needlessly closer to her prompted her to shift her bag to hang in front.

A train arrived heading towards Alem. A train for Los Incas arrived so full that she passed on it after she saw the boys press into it.

The live music was pleasant enough. She resisted the desire to sway along; it just wasn't done. No foot tapping, finger drumming or singing along either, not in Buenos Aires.

After two trains towards Alem, the next train towards Los Incas arrived. She pushed on and grabbed a seat between two men. She had never gotten a seat this early in a ride home. The middle-aged man to her left was a professional, she surmised by the quality of his black shoes, black overcoat and scarf of muted tones; he had his subway face—*su Subte cara*—fixed. He held a Borge anthology open in one hand and made no acknowledgment of her presence. To her right was an older man who smiled weakly at her, nodded and mumbled a *buonas tardes* to her. He had sad, beaten eyes. Like so many others, his skin was pale and waxy—too much city life and hours in commute to look healthy during the winter. His clothes, all in shades of brown, were as worn as his face. Already uncomfortably wedged into the last seat of the bench, he tried to make a little more space for Marisol. By the time the train moved, he had closed his eyes, pretending to sleep.

At the next station, dozens more joined them. Like everyone else, she chose to ignore the three older women who got on at the next stop. By law, relinquishing one's seat was only required for pregnant women and the handicapped. They didn't look like either; ergo, no need to offer.

Most people remained bundled up in spite of the heat building in the car; it was wintertime, after all. She watched a drop of sweat trail down the temple of the man to her left. He moved, ever so slightly, to indicate that he was aware of her glance and that he was not pleased. She unbuttoned her coat and loosened her scarf and mumbled an *excúseme* to the man on her right whom she jostled with her elbow. He kept his eyes closed and gave the slightest snort of *no problema*.

They traveled onward, stopping at one point inside the tunnel for several stuffy, silent minutes. Through a jumble of coat sleeves, bags and fingers tensed around iPods or cell phones or Palm Pilots, she watched a pickpocket reach into someone's bag. She could not be sure whether she was actually witnessing a theft, so she said nothing.

The man on the right gave a snort then a sigh. She glanced over at him, joining the collective glare from those who had heard him. She watched him for a long while after others turned back to their earbuds, their unfocused stares, their own little worlds.

More people squeezed on. She felt the press of a woman in a heavy gray overcoat against her knees, more grateful than ever to have gotten a seat. She stared into the gray wool. A jerky departure at the next station mildly surprised the chattering crones standing nearby. No one else reacted.

She turned her gaze back to the man in brown. Something was different. His eyes no longer twitched under his eyelids. His jaw had slackened. His pale skin looked even waxier. She studied his chest for signs of movement. None. She leaned in ever so slightly to listen for breathing. Nothing.

Another station came and went. More passengers left than jammed on. Another station and another. The crones were gone.

With the jostle of another departure, the man-in-brown's hand slid off of his lap and touched hers. It was cold, already cold. She picked it up by the edge of the sleeve and placed it back on his thigh. No one noticed a thing. The jerk of the car pulling away again threatened to repeat the motion, but the hand stayed put. The man's head bobbled slightly between the window behind them and the dull aluminum tubing bracing his right side.

She stared blankly towards his feet and clutched her bag tightly as though it was the only real thing in the entire car. To her left, a young man in black replaced the middle-aged man in black. The crowd thinned with each of the remaining stations. The young man in black was replaced by the woman in gray. With each start and stop, she convinced herself anew that the quiet man to her right was simply asleep.

She felt a mild tug of the slowing train. It was her stop, Tronador station. She stood, expecting to see the man adjust— Slump? Fall? Stand? Wink? She looked at him a moment longer, still debating whether she should cry out, "¡Él es muerto! He's dead!" But it was too late. She had waited too long to act. She would have just looked stupid if she said anything now. She didn't have time to report anything, not tonight. She did have the date of sorts with the manager of the cafe. No, she didn't have to concern herself with the man on the *Subte*. Someone would take care of it eventually.

The doors slid open and she stepped out. And that's when she knew she'd have no problem finishing the internship.

About the author:

A mathematician by degree, a musician by choice, a mom by—well, we all know the usual way one gets to be a mom—Jean Tschohl Quinn feels that she doesn't so much write stories or compose music as much as have them occur to her. This story will be her third appearance in a Scribes Valley anthology. One of her stories also appears in Under the Rose by Norilana Press. Other than that, she tries to make music, serve her community and generally avoid housework. She lives with her husband, three daughters who are flying the nest with startling rapidity, two old dogs and some fruit trees in the Redwoods along the Central Coast of California.

Ya Baha'ul'Abha!

THE EYE OF THE BEHOLDER
©2010 by George Thomas

Fifty-five-year-old Gregor Capek interrupted his friend's defense of Ellen Stone's sanity. "Nonsense, Alan, she's deranged!"

Facing Gregor on a weather-beaten bench, Alan Kindermann frowned. "My dear Gregor, you don't have to yell." Glancing around the dogwood-dotted grounds of the private mental institution, he pulled at his ear. "We're lucky everyone is at lunch so we won't be overheard." He ran a pudgy hand through his disheveled hair. Fifteen years younger than his friend, he still dared to bait him. His eyes twinkled. "Just remember, madness is in the eye of the beholder."

Gregor's eyebrows shot up. "Don't be absurd, Alan! Her actions shout insanity! It's not just *my* opinion that brought her here."

Alan, irritated by this dead-end conversation, felt warm and sticky, even in the shade of the magnolia tree. He slouched and mopped his forehead with a grubby handkerchief, then shook his head. "Gregor, with your classic education and training, it's no wonder you find Ellen's world abnormal."

The older man glared and thrust out his chin. "Quite, quite. But we know that mental illness alienates people from society. Ellen Stone is alienated—schizophrenic, in a word."

Alan cringed. "Come now, my dear friend. Schizophrenia is one of those old-fashioned social labels. It's unfair to imprison people here because society doesn't like them. You know very well that locked up in this place year after year away from the real world and real responsibilities, people can forget how to cope. They become dependent on others for all their needs, doomed to an institution for the rest of their lives." He shuddered. "That's starting to happen to Ellen Stone. We must not let it!"

Gregor stiffened. "Remember, it's dangerous to get upset about the patients. Let's stick to the facts. You must have noticed Ellen's withdrawal during last Saturday's group therapy session. And she scribbles all the time, as if she were taking notes. She carries that confounded clipboard with her everywhere. I've even seen her scratching on it during lunch! I asked to see what she'd written. But she snatched it away."

"Perhaps she just wanted privacy."

Gregor slapped his knee. "She has a compulsion for privacy. And what about her clothes? That same drab, shapeless dress, day after day. With those ugly oxford shoes! Is it normal for a pretty young girl to dress that way? I tried joking with her about it the other day." He sniffed. "She became prissy and told me it was her uniform. Uniform! Why, she's in another world half the time, I tell you." Gregor uncrossed his legs and flicked an imaginary speck from his trousers. "In addition," he ticked off on his fingers, "she schedules her days to the minute, bosses everyone around, avoids close contact with anyone...I could go on and on."

Alan sighed. To him, making judgments about someone's personality by examining a few fragments of it was like looking at individual bricks and trying to determine the character of a house. He felt his damp, wrinkled suit cling to his round body. His chin itched and he rubbed his whiskers. "My dear friend, I grant you that Ellen Stone is different, even eccentric. Still, we all have delusions. Hers may be more extreme than ours. But if she lived on the outside, would people find her more bizarre than the rest out there?"

Gregor threw up his hands. "See, you, it would be unfair to *her* if we discharged her. She'd go to pieces under any pressure or stress. I'm sorry, Alan, but she's got to remain here longer."

A door slammed in the nearest building. Ellen Stone appeared and gazed around. Gregor whispered, "There she is now, looking for us, I'll wager."

She spotted them and strode their way along a graceful, curving sidewalk. "There you are! *Tch*, *tch*, gentlemen. You've nearly talked right through the lunch hour. Shouldn't you have something to eat?"

Gregor fired a knowing look at his younger friend. He bowed slightly toward Ellen. "If you'll feel better, Miss Stone, we'll have lunch."

She stood ramrod straight and watched them stroll down an azalea-bordered sidewalk toward the open dining room where both staff and the more rational patients dined together.

That evening, as the street lamps winked on around the manicured grounds, Alan stepped into a large paneled living room where he found Gregor playing chess with a patient. A young night attendant burst through the door. "Has anyone seen Doc Swenson?"

Doc, a patient in his early 80s and not a doctor at all, had been institutionalized as long as anyone could remember. Bordering on senility but perfectly harmless, he occasionally wandered off and forgot where he was. The old man hadn't been seen since lunch when he'd signed himself out for the afternoon.

Alan sprang up, a stab of fear catching him in the chest. He remembered that Doc had taken to wandering to Brewster Lake, a small, deep, spring-fed body of water on the grounds. Moreover, Doc had recently mumbled about feeling worthless, and had even talked of suicide.

Alan could see that similar thoughts raced through Gregor's mind. The older man leaped up, raced after the attendant, and snapped, "While we're gone, call on Miss Stone if you need any assistance."

The young man peered at Gregor with an odd expression. "But Miss Stone left half an hour ago to look for Doc!"

Gregor shot Alan a wild look and they both ran for the door. The young man protested and rushed after them. Alan yelled over his shoulder as the two men plunged out into the night, "No, no. You stay here—we'll go."

A bright full moon vividly etched all details of the landscape. Both men jogged the short distance to the lake. Arriving out of breath, Alan grabbed Gregor's arm. "Look, the gate's open and there are two people on that dock."

When they reached the foot of the pier, they could make out the features of the two people. Doc sat close to the far end. Ellen stood a few feet away. In the quiet clear night, the two men could hear Ellen and Doc arguing.

Doc slumped over. "I'm no use. I have no family, no friends, nothing to live for."

Ellen spoke, firm and authoritative. "We're *more* than your friends, Doc. We're your family and you're *our* family. How would we get along without you? What would Mrs. Mitchell do without you to read to her? Who would organize the bingo games? How would we keep track of our weekly schedules without your help?" She stepped closer. "How can you possibly say you're useless? You're the most important person on that entire ward."

Doc wavered. "Do you think so?"

"I *know* so. You have more experience than anyone else there. We depend on you to keep things going. No more talk of doing away with yourself."

"Well..."

She took the old man's arm and helped him to his feet. "C'mon, let's go home now."

Alan blurted, "Thank goodness you're both safe! Good work, Miss Stone. You saved Doc's life."

Ellen whirled. "What are you two doing here?" She sputtered at them as they all started back.

Once again in the living room, Alan poked his older friend in the chest. "Well, what do you think about Ellen Stone now?"

Gregor thought for a minute then slapped his knees and sprang up. "Alan, you've been right all along. I was wrong. There's no point in delaying any longer. I'll tell her now."

Ellen stood talking with the attendant and scribbling on her clipboard when Gregor pulled her aside. "Miss Stone, we've concluded that you're ready now for a full discharge. Your level-headed action tonight with Doc convinced us."

She stared at him then flashed a little smile. "Why, thank you. That's wonderful news. Er, would you come with me for a moment, please?"

They walked together to the glassed-in office of the ward, where Ellen slipped a key out of her olive-green nurse's uniform and unlocked the medicine cabinet on the wall. She flipped through the sheets of paper on her clipboard until she reached the one labeled 'Medications.' Running her finger down the list of patient names, she stopped at the entry

Gregor R. Capek, Room 35 – 10 milligrams Haloperidol, orally once daily before retiring

Taking a bottle from the cabinet, she turned toward Gregor. "In all the excitement, Mr. Capek, I almost forgot to give you and Mr. Kindermann your medications."

About the author:

Post-college, after a five-year stint in the US Navy and four years programming with IBM, George Thomas worked thirty-one years in Finance for Xerox Corporation in upstate New York and southern Connecticut, with foreign assignments in France and Mexico. After retiring to western Florida, he started watercolor painting and writing short stories, instructed in both fields by many great Sarasota teachers. He has entered many short story contests, winning awards in a few. He is currently revising a novel.

He and his wife enjoy the rich Sarasota cultural environment and the many available volunteering opportunities. They travel often, abroad as well as to Phoenix and San Francisco to visit children and grandchildren.

A LITTLE DOG SHALL LEAD THEM
©2010 by Diana Thurbon

He shall gather them together into a place...called
ARMAGEDDON. And there were...sounds of
thunder...and the great city was divided.
(Rev. 16-19)

He wakes to the drizzle of water in a down pipe—that's how he knows he's dreaming. It must be ten years since the heavy dark red clouds that float across the asbestos sky drizzled anything other than dust. Jack forces his eyes open. The desiccated dawn fills the sky with a greenish hue. He struggles to the bathroom—it feels hot already. Careful not to waste a drop of water, he cleans his teeth almost dry and spits salt, brushes the dust from his dark blonde hair and spends a moment looking in the dusty cracked mirror. Tired blue eyes. He looks old and worn. Yet he's not either, not really. He takes a long, centring breath. He's ready to spend a day checking their fortifications.

He sees himself as a dream keeper. It was never his War, his Storm, but he's determined to build a brighter future from the mess. His wife is making rattling sounds in the kitchen. He knows what food is left. He doesn't want any of it. He calls to her, "Nothing for me, thanks. Be there in a minute."

It's a grey, forsaken and ugly world. Clouds of acrid smelling dust billow across the little cabin. She waits for it to settle and then sweeps it away, submerging herself in reassuring routine. He walks into the kitchen, she removes her face mask and he kisses her goodbye. She puts the broom down, sniffs and hands him a flask of the precious filtered water. "Be careful."

"Of course," he says. "You, too."

"You know I always am." She glances instinctively to their back room, filled now with books. Jack follows her gaze. It's taken a long time to find so many. He doesn't like leaving her, but he needs to protect their boundaries and to continue his search for the knowledge. He collects disks, too, though for the moment they can't play them. Most days he finds something they can eat.

Sarah knows her role is vital. She starts sorting by subject. Before the Storm she had been a librarian: data is everything. It's their hope for a fresh start. First, she wants to organise all the information they can find.

She catalogues knowledge as he brings it home. The task is daunting so she tries to stay in the moment. Histories, battles, philosophy, poetry and psychology; then computing, mathematics, biology, science, engineering and technology. Job by job, day by day, she tries not to think far ahead.

Jack wishes he could drive. There are vehicles left, but no fuel. It's slow without wheels. He feels like an eagle with clipped wings. He steps into the doorway and reconnoitres the nearby wastelands. The terrain is indistinguishable from yesterday—all the yesterdays. The morning star is low in the sky. Seven hundred million miles away, he remembers that from school. "Look Sarah, it's iridescent green today."

They watch. It gradually disappears below the soft greyish horizon and the hot sun slowly rises to shine again.

Somehow that other world so far away cheers him up. He imagines a people living in harmony and friendship. *If only.* "I'm off now."

"Goodbye, then, see you when you get back."

Eight kilometres away over the rubble and the formidable, dark, smouldering canyon that divides them, Jaya is in his morning room writing. His partner, Fayin, nurses her sucking, happily farting baby and watches Jaya fill page after page with diagrams and paragraphs of neat, small script.

She misses her own science: botany. "Hah—what botany? Plants are few. What could I study? Thistles and other hardy herbs, cape weed and a few fungi."

Jaya is an engineer. He is struggling to find a way forward.

"It must be hard...no computer." Then, "Stupid Cow!" She silently curses herself for mouthing redundant stupidity.

"I need more data, much more, and it *is* slow without a computer. But the dust would wreck a computer anyway." He doesn't want to whinge—that's a slippery slope to nowhere. "Is Jay-son keeping guard already? It's not even dawn yet."

"Yes."

Jay-son is their other child, now sixteen, almost a man; he survived the Storm with his parents.

"Don't leave him alone too long, Fayin."

"He'll be all right, but I'll join him after we put the baby down. She looks out the window. "What a beautiful starset."

He walks over to the window. There's not much dust this early; the wind hasn't risen yet. He stands beside her and gazes at the large star slowly falling below the smudged horizon. "It looks so green this morning. Do you suppose it's covered in grass? It may be inhabited."

She laughs at him. "Fat chance, Jaya, but yesterday morning it looked blue so maybe it is covered in water."

"Then it would have an atmosphere, wouldn't it? Water would evaporate."

Shrugging, she hands him the baby, and goes out into Barren to keep watch with their son. The heavy heat presses down on her.

On the other side of the Barren, across the perilous canyon, Sarah is looking through a large, illustrated book Jack has found—only the cover has been damaged. It is full of big coloured maps and gloriously coloured pictures of a rainbow world of blues and shades of greens and ochres. She looks at a large map showing the distributions of different religions.

She reflects, *There should be one Spirit that people call what they will. No person ought to claim a perfect religion. People used to affirm absolute truth and that others were wrong because they had different rituals. That's how it started.* She pauses and remembers. *Faith attacked faith and didn't allow the other to be. If no one is harmed or coerced, religion could provide a moral compass that brings peace instead of Storm.* Why couldn't they see that?

It had been an insane game. The participants had been both the predators and the prey. Ultimately it had been lethal. She shakes her head, puts the heavy book away and begins to sort a variety of computer technology books.

Fayin clambers through the crumbling rubble and smoldering ash down to Jay-son. She sees he is covered in the dust and ash; unable to escape the ever-relentless sun, his sweat is running in grey trickles down his face. He looks frantic, "Mom I've lost our little lion dog. I can't find him. He chased a rat that came out of the drain and ran into the canyon. I've been calling him and searching for more than an hour. He might have fallen into a shaft or a fire. What if he gets to the other side? They'll eat him, won't they?"

She reaches out to her son, "I'm afraid so, Jay-son. They are savages and they will be hungry just as we are."

"Well, we are hungry but we didn't eat him when he crawled out of the dust wagging his tail."

"But we aren't savages, and they are."

"Dad says they sacrifice animals to their god. How could...we have to find him, Mum."

"Jay-son, they have big walls—barriers they guard. He won't get through and at suppertime he'll come home to us." She sends her son to wash off the poisonous dust.

He returns and sits on a smooth, black heat-blasted rock beside her. They both peer down the canyon hoping to see Lowchen. All day they wait and watch for the Others and watch, too, for Lowchen.

Jack has finished his long morning patrolling. He has done two thirds of the barricade line and has made one incursion into the crumbling black vacuum but has found only a few computer disks in rubble, sadly none of the precious printed books or papers today.

He passes a garbage dump where bodies have been burned. He trips over a skull and falls in the ash. Standing up and brushing himself off, he looks around. He can see the whiteness of long limb bones and the shape of grey skulls peering through ash with sightless eyes. He turns his head away and shudders. He wishes he could protect Sarah from the horror.

Back at the cabin he hands his wife a small bunch of thistles and fungi.

She says, "You look exhausted. I wish I could help."

"You *are* helping and I want you to stay right out of it. Out of the sludge and ash dumps...until after the baby. It's no place...."

"Maybe it's too late. Maybe it doesn't matter. Maybe our baby already has two heads, or webbed hands and feet, or feathers, or no mouth or no eyes. Maybe we are all zombies playing out a meaningless horror show—"

"Stop it!" he interrupts sharply; his own fears are momentarily exposed by his sudden anger.

"I'm sorry, but sometimes the idea of a whole life in this septic, scabbed land is overwhelming, let alone bequeathing it to a child. And how do we know our child will ever find anyone and not be alone forever?"

"Sarah, we have to keep hope alive. *Shh*! What's that noise?"

"I didn't hear anything."

"Listen...an animal sound."

"Probably a rat," she says.

"No, it sounded like a...listen!"

Wuf Wuf

"A dog!" she is incredulous. "We've searched for animals and searched. We've only ever found a few snakes, some rodents and the dust grubs."

"There it is again."

Wuf Wuf

Jack and Sarah run outside together. In the yard looking up at them is a very small grey dog the colour of the dust. He runs over to them and sits expectantly.

"Poor thing." Sarah scoops him up with one hand. They go inside and put the tiny dog down on a box. He shakes himself and sulphurous grey dust particles thicken the air. Sarah runs to get her small battery-powered dust remover and wet brush. Jack goes out to their food store to see what might suit a small, hungry dog.

He returns ten minutes later with a meal cake and a few cold-boiled dust grubs. Sarah meanwhile has been hard at work. The little dog is a creamy white and silver grey. His evenly scissored coat shines silvery in the luminescent sunlight glimmering through the dusty window. He cocks his perky fold-over ears and his wide hazel eyes gaze trustingly at them. Round his neck is a hand-platted red and green collar. There is a ring on the collar and attached to the ring is a little silver horseshoe encrusted with sparkling diamonds. Jack reaches out to gently finger the soft collar. A tiny pink tongue appears from below a little button black nose and licks Jack's hand. Sarah crumbles the cake into a dish for their visitor and Jack goes outside.

He returns fifteen minutes later. "There is a small hole in the base of the wall. He's come from across the canyon. He must belong to the Others."

Sarah is amazed. "But they are the savages. Wouldn't they eat him or sacrifice him? Look, it doesn't make sense. He's a *pet*!"

Jack frowns. "The little dog is small and helpless, yet he has no fear. He's been looked after and treated kindly. We've been wrong Sarah. We have been making the same mistake people made before the Storm. We've let mistrust and the fear of difference harden our own hearts."

She frowns and shakes her head. "So? Living like this would close any heart."

"Only if we let it, Sarah. That's what caused the Storm. Yes, it's hard not to behave the same way; we still feel fear and mistrust. Yet we have a duty. This land isn't ours. We are the custodians and builders for tomorrow."

"Fancy talk. I know you believe that, but the Storm generations killed each other. Shouldn't we be careful?"

"That doesn't mean we are doomed to that kind of life."

"Ha! They clotted our rivers with the dead. Now our water is poisoned."

"And should we perpetuate this for our child, Sarah? Look at the little dog. He is cared for and happy. His owners must be good people. They must be. Nothing else is rational. This is our chance to begin to create a compassionate world. Or do we want the future to repeat the same nightmare?"

"Of course we don't, Jack, but what the hell are you saying?"

"We are going to take him home."

"Are you nuts?" Her eyes widen and she looks stunned. "Go through our barrier and across that terrible canyon to them? It's crumbling and unstable, it's full of craters and in places the ash is still burning."

"I've never been more serious. It's our only hope. We'll be careful. We will carry the little dog. I'll make a white flag to wave and we will talk in the Universal Language to tell them we have brought back their dog."

Sarah slowly nods, but she looks scared as she reaches down and fondles the dog's ears.

Fayin and Jay-son have given up. Off and on all day, they have called the little dog. Jaya has now joined them, the baby on his back "The moon wind is rising. You are late for supper. I could smell hot ash on the wind. I was worried about you."

"We've lost Lowchen. He ran into the canyon. We've waited as long as we dared. We hoped he'd return, we've been sick with worry. Maybe he's dust bound and can't climb out."

"Oh no! I'm sorry, Fayin, but it's almost dark, it's dangerous, we have to go back. We will search tomorrow."

Jay-son shouts, "Mom, what's that?" He points, they can just make out two people climbing over the darkening canyon rim. They are holding up a white flag. The man seems to be carrying a small parcel. They watch open-mouthed as the couple slowly makes their way toward them, and then stop. The man bends down and places his gift—or whatever it is—on the ground. The parcel morphs into their little lion dog and he bounds towards them and leaps into Jay-son's arms. The two couples tentatively approach each other.

"We found your dog," Jack carefully enunciates.

"Thank you," says Jaya and slowly extends his hand.

Jack takes it and the men look into each other's eyes.

The women stare at each other for a moment, then Fayin says, "Thank you."

"He is so tiny and cute," says Sarah, "you must love him to bits."

"Yes," says Fayin. "There is not much left that is good to love. We were so lucky to find Lowchen one hundred starsets ago."

"Looks like he was lucky that you did," Sarah says, looking at the little dog in his master's arms. His tail is wagging furiously and his lips are curled up in a doggy smile.

It is dawn. The four adults have been up all night talking and forging their plans for a new future of shared work, friendship and harmony. Jay-son, though, has sat cuddling the dog and not saying much. All are sitting quiet now, emotionally spent and for the moment talked out. They all are aware a new dream is beginning. The luminous green star is filling the horizon and they gaze quietly mesmerized as its shimmering beauty is illuminated by the rising sun.

"The third planet from the sun!" says Sarah.

"Yes," says Fayin. "Do you think there are people on that world?

I wonder if they live in peace and share unifying dreams."

"Perhaps! I think that they may," says Jack. "Their planet is still green and blue, not like the grey dust bowl we have created here. We razed and ruined our world, but that is the past. Now we will pool our skills in harmony and start again."

The others nod in agreement.

Jay-son speaks up, "I know you'll think I'm young but I'm strong. One of us must explore the beyond and search for survivors. You know it has to be me. You all have work here. I have a special quest, too. I will find another dog. Lowchen has brought us together so I shall find a mate for him." He turns and smiles at Jack and Sarah. "And one day my family will give your family a puppy."

Lowchen looks up to his master and wags his generous tail, *Wuf Wuf*.

The shining green planet slips below the horizon and a new day dawns.

About the author:

Diana Thurbon is post 60, with adult children who are more grown up than she is, and some delightful grown and almost grown grandchildren. She lives in the southeast "burbs" of Melbourne, Australia with her flying instructor/pilot/writer husband, her cranky cocker spaniel, Anakin, and two idiosyncratic crater digging hens, Orphan Annie (a rescue hen) and Emily.

Diana used to be a librarian but changed careers after a serious bout with lymphoma and a bone marrow transplant. Now she teaches meditation and writes. She also boards holidaying dogs and sometimes she tries out her work by reading aloud to them and the resident spaniel. Mostly they fall asleep.

Writing has always been part of who she is and lately she spends more and more time pursuing this part of her life. Her fiction is mostly a kind of gentle magic realism and, despite an awfully idiosyncratic approach to punctuation, a number of her stories and poems have been published in Australia and on the

Internet. She also is a keen literary contest writer and has won firsts in several competitions. Her writing is mostly suitable for Human Beings to read. When she finishes a story and reads it, she likes to enjoy it. She always hopes her readers will respond the same way.

DUCK YOU
©2010 by Denise C. Hengeli

Quack Queek! Low flying birds announcing spring.

Larry bends down to avoid being brushed by wings. He shakes his fist. "Damn birds, get away!"

Ignoring his threat, the birds come closer and the sea gull's gray wings expand to ride a breeze in a graceful turn, as a fat-bellied duck flaps to keep up.

"Strange pair! Sea gull and duck. Looks like the duck is in flight training. Fat thing, he is. If he had a tongue it would be hangin' out pantin', he's workin' that hard. Crappin' damn birds. Wish they'd both fly into the side of a buildin'."

Quack Queek

"Should have known. The duck's a she, makin' all the noise. She ain't carrying eggs. Just one of the fat ones. Her webbed feet can't tuck into her sides. Kinda like me," he smiles.

Approaching his fiftieth birthday, Larry has given up exercise and lately realizes his pear-shaped belly hides what he considers his most appealing body part. Unfortunately, his wife Sarah doesn't agree. His sex life has become a memory.

Wheezing as he completes a long-delayed chore of removing storm windows from his aging house, Larry acknowledges his depression. "Another winter gone and thank God it's over. I can tolerate the heat, but the cold gets deeper into my bones each year."

Carrying the storm windows to the garage, he sees bird

droppings on the windows he just washed. "No sooner clean than dirty again. Gonna' shoot them birds someday. Soon as it warms, the damned birds eat and crap. I think they like to aim for my head."

Walking across his lawn, dormant from winter winds, he opens his front door wondering where his wife is. He sees the tips of her slippers as she sits in her favorite lounge chair.

"Sarah? Sarah? Goin' down to the docks to watch the boats." Grumbling, he warns, "The birds are comin' out again now that it's warmer. Comin' too close to all them cages you have in the side yard. Got to get away from birds for a while. Hate birds. All kinds. Gonna' relax and watch the water."

Showing no interest, Sarah watches him climb into his six-year-old car, push the AC button and roll the windows down.

"My little exercise of rebellion," he calls. "Air conditioning and open car windows. I'll cool the world!"

Thirteen years of married misery have sharpened Larry and Sarah. Each believes life would be peaceful if only the other would change annoying habits. Dreaming of having things he can't afford, Larry makes no attempt to lessen his yearnings for expensive items even though his salary as a shoe salesman does not support his yearnings. Bitter words flew from Sarah over the huge surround-sound television he installed in the room he calls his "theater." Sarah is not a television fan, preferring nurturing of her personal hobbies of breeding and training birds. She sees only excess in over-sized televisions. She shuns luxuries; considers herself a saver. Saves paper, food scraps, small buttons, ribbons and feathers. She raises pigeons, ducks and an occasional sea gull. She spends hours training the birds to fly and it's Larry's opinion that she can train them to crap just as they fly over his head.

Driving to the town docks that Larry calls his yacht club, he exits his car to walk along the water's edge. Hitching his pants, he turns his attention to a boat glistening in the sunlight. "Imagine owning such a boat! My life would be complete. I could get away from Sarah and her stinkin' birds."

His grin looks evil and he jumps when he hears: "Mornin'!" A man extends his hand. "Beauty ain't she? How are you this fine mornin'? I'm who they call 'Bob the Boat Bargainer.' What they say, yes sir."

Both men duck as a pair of low flying birds brush their heads.

"Man! Birds are wild this mornin'. What's that? A sea gull and duck? Never seen them paired in flight like that."

"Just thinkin' the same thing."

As he steers Larry left, Bob chatters, "Let's go in my office before they decorate our hair with leftover breakfast." Adjusting his silk shirt Bob opens the door to his sales office, pours brandy-coffee sludge into dingy cups and hands one to Larry. "Plain coffee ain't never enough, know what I mean? Let's have an eye-opener." He adds more brandy.

Rocking on his heels, Bob promises, "Make you a great deal on that honey of a boat! Just got her this mornin'. Ain't she got a sweet body? Sweet as a good woman. If you're thinkin' to buy, I got papers right here. You can be ridin' this afternoon. Fifteen grand floats you away."

As Larry's stomach churns from the brandy, he hides his excitement. *What a deal! Bob's givin' me a great price!* Again, hitching his pants, Larry takes a deep breath and lets it whistle through his front teeth. "Got to talk with the little woman, ya' know?" He pokes the salesman in his side. "I call her little but that ain't so. She's bigger than the wide side of a barn. Tell ya' 'bout her. The wife's a bird-keeper. Keeps birds. Pigeons mostly. Saves bread to feed ducks. Hate all them things. Even seen a sea gull in the yard eatin' from her hand."

Bob becomes restless. *Who cares 'bout the wife? Just buy the damned boat*, he thinks. He tries to look interested in Larry's story, imagining the vacation he'll take if he can just sell this boat.

"She's gonna hate me havin' a boat, so maybe we'll be even. She'll hate the boat, I hate her birds. Be back soon. Don't let anyone buy that boat."

Bob settles back into his chair and puts his feet on the edge of a rusted desk. *Last sale I had was jet skis for chrissakes. Got to close a sale to this guy.* He reaches under his desk and pokes though chunks of ice in his cooler for his bottle of vodka. He up-ends the bottle and lets his throat bathe in a long drink. *This is the good stuff. Got to settle down and make a sale to this guy who looks like a candidate for cardiac arrest. A wife trainin' birds. Whoever heard of that?*

As Larry leaves Bob's office two birds rise from their perch on a high post and steer into his path. "What the hell? The same two birds? Gonna' chase me home, you crappin' birds?" Sliding into the front seat of his car Larry wishes the seat belt wasn't so tight. "Got to get exercisin' so I can move better on that boat. Let myself go flabby, but I got a whole year before I turn fifty, so I'll lose fifty pounds. One for each year. All I gotta do is get Sarah to agree to ownin' a boat."

With increasing nervousness, he thinks about Sarah's reaction to this purchase. He enters his driveway and sees it's marked with green and white bird droppings. "Man, bird crap all over."

Uneasy about seeing Sarah, Larry stands at the kitchen door and calls, "Sarah, come here. Got news! I'm buyin' a boat!"

He hears Sarah shout from another room. "You're kiddin', right?" Entering the kitchen carrying duck feathers, she waves her arms and begins to rant. "Great! Terrific! Past due bills piled everywhere and you wanna' buy a boat? What the hell for? You spend, spend, spend."

Softer now. "If it was a houseboat you'd live on and be gone from here, I'd buy the damn' thing for you. But no. No way. Can't afford it, don't want it, can't get it, and that's that. You think, dream, and talk of trash to buy. What crap! No way! Fergit' it!"

Larry follows her from room to room as her voice rises in pitch with each word until she pushes past him, opening the kitchen door, letting it slam hard enough to rattle the windows. He watches her cross the yard to her thirteen pigeon coops, where the *coo-coo* of her birds can be heard.

"She calls what I want crap? It's her birds that are crap!"

He watches her open a cage door to whisper, "Oooo, my wittle woves, Mommy's here." She pokes a manicured finger through narrow bars. "Stupid wants a boat. Silly, silly man. Imagine!" Stroking her pigeons' fragile backs with a light touch, Sarah flicks away bird droppings, ignoring a smear on her hand. "Wets get you cagey open so you can fwy, my tweets." Sarah opens cage doors one-by-one.

At the kitchen window, Larry watches with disgust as the trees become loaded with pigeons of all colors and sizes. "Listen to that stupid talk! They're birds for chrissakes! Pigeons! What a moron."

Tree branches and roots become decorated with frosting-like bird droppings.

"Ewww," he mutters. "Disgustin'. Look at her fussin'. Stinkin' birds have no good use."

Sarah waves a wand above the birds to scatter them out over the neighborhood as Larry's fury increases. She bends down and picks up a feather with a blunt end. She opens a small container and adds her new feather to a pile of feathers mixed with bits of bread.

"This one will be for my special treat. Savin' all the feathers."

Sarah's temper is cooled by the thought of her neighbor Jim and her devotion to their weekly courtship. Sarah discovered Jim has a sexual feather fetish and she encourages and satisfies his twisted longings as they make love in a most unusual way. She trails feather-ends over his body until he's screaming for release, then scratches the sharp ends of feathers over his back until he convulses with perverse pleasure. He's become part of her plan to free herself from her dull marriage. She smiles, imagining their next meeting when she'll present new feathers to Jim.

"I'll enslave him."

Sarah doesn't particularly enjoy her meetings with Jim. *His only imagination is an unusual use of feathers*, she thinks. *But he amuses me, and I will put his desire for our meetings to good use.*

Moving to the open kitchen door, Larry decides, "I can't stand anymore bird crap. My car's never free of smears. I've got to get away from these birds."

Bolting out the door, Larry ignores a screen that falls to the ground. He climbs into his car. "I want that boat, dammit. Got to get me away from her and her damned birds. Who in hell does she think she is? She can't tell me what not to do!"

Slamming his foot onto the gas pedal, he burns rubber marks on the driveway. As though on cue, two overhead pigeons drop white trails down his windshield. "Crap! Crap! Crap! I can't keep it off my car!" Jerking hard on the windshield wiper handle squirts fluid on the birds' mess creating a smeared white arc. Squinting through the mess he moans, "Can't even see through the stinkin' stuff. Gotta' outrun this mess."

Back at the docks, Larry's car skids into a parking space. Stepping out of his car he slips on a wet blob left by the overhead sea gull. The next second, the duck squirts green specks on his arm. "Birds! Ever-crappin' birds!"

Entering Bob's office, Larry hears a bell ring in a back office and calls, "Bob! Let's go! I'm gettin' that boat. Gimme' the papers and I'll be outa' here."

"Glad to see you back! The little lady agreed to buy the boat, eh?" Bob thumps Larry's back with approval.

"Hell, no! Boatin's my thing! Her thing is bitchin'. That and messin' with her stinkin' birds. Know anything about pigeons? Most crappin' birds you'll ever see!" Larry leans over papers, signs with a flourish.

Dangling a set of boat keys, left, right, left, right, in front of Larry's nose, Bob announces, "All set. The keys to your dream."

Grabbing the keys, Larry rushes out of the sales office into sunshine dancing off the bow of his "yacht". It's not big enough to be called "yacht," but it's his, and he'll call it whatever he wants. The boat rises with the movement of water lapping dockside. Noticing bird droppings on the side of the boat he grabs a nearby rag and brushes them off. "Ever stinkin' birds! They're everywhere!"

Giddy with joy, Larry steps into the boat and brings the boat motors to life. Taking off trappings of land, he empties his pockets of wallet, cell phone, and car keys, putting them in a storage box tucked under a seat. Loosening his belt two holes, he breathes ocean air, letting his belly relax. Pushing back thoughts about his small paycheck, he rationalizes, "If Sarah would stop buyin' those crappin' birds, we'd have enough money to pay our bills."

Larry hears the rumble of the motor as he backs the boat out of its slip. "What a boat. A beauty for sure."

Spotting his neighbor Jim lounging by water's edge, Larry calls, "Jim, look! Here she is! She shines, gleams, I can smell her newness!"

Jim prances alongside the boat as it glides to the end of the dock. "Where'd you get it Larry? Where ya going?"

"Just bought her. Listen to her growl. Want a first ride in the boat of my dreams?"

"Sure, get closer and I'll jump in." *Damn! Somethin' else he got first.* Jim's been Larry's neighbor for eight long years, envying all he has. Larry's house is bigger, his car newer, his vacations longer, his wife sexier. He used to envy Larry's marriage to Sarah until he discovered he can have Friday visits with her, receiving body massages blended with her inventive and powerful style of sexual pleasure. Jim's feelings of second-best fade as Sarah soothes his feelings of inadequacy. He's hooked by her use of duck feathers to trail over his body until he screams his pleasure. At his moment of surrender, she scratches hard ends of feathers down his back- marking tracks he carries with pride.

The only thing that could improve my Friday fun is letting Larry know about Sarah and me. The thought fuels Jim's desire. Leaping into Larry's boat, Jim thinks, *Another thing of his to envy.*

"How fast can she go, Larry?"

"Don't know. Let's find out."

Larry throttles the motor, easing the boat away from the dock through no-wake zones. Turning into open water he gives a dramatic wave of his hand, opens the motor to a faster gear as Jim stumbles with the initial leap of the boat.

"It's mine! Hey, world, look what I've got!"

With increasing speed, the boat skims the water as the men react to its power.

"Hold on, pal. This baby moves!" Larry gloats.

Rub it in now, Jim thinks. *I'll rub it in Sarah Friday.*

The boat bathes her hull in the water, creating very little wake. Admiring the vastness of the open water, Larry notices a bird frantically flapping its wings in an effort to catch up with the speeding boat.

Squinting through sunshine, Larry says, "It's a duck. Again? The same duck? Couldn't be. Man, I hate all kinds of birds, ducks included. Their crap is bigger than Sarah's pigeons, and they don't care where they drop a load. Watch this. This slick sweetheart will out-race any bird, pigeon or duck."

With the motor set at full speed, the boat darts forward. Looking back at the bird, Larry realizes the duck is getting closer. Catching up with the boat, it slows its flapping and hovers directly overhead, staying even with the boat's speed.

"Let's get out from under this thing before it lets loose and messes in the boat. Looks like the duck from this mornin' wearing itself out to annoy me."

Larry changes the boat's direction, but the duck adjusts its speed and direction, staying overhead. A sudden *Quack-Queek* makes the two men glance at each other and laugh.

"I think it just called you a geek," Jim teases.

"Not me. Sarah's the geek, not me! She's the one who loves birds, all birds. She makes me as sick as birds do!" Clenching his jaw with fury, Larry waves his fist at the low flying bird. "Get away! Git! Go on!"

The bird stays overhead.

"Damn stupid bird! I know it's a 'she,' it's that stubborn!"

With a slight movement of tail-feathers, the bird releases a yellow-green blob, splattering Larry's glistening boat deck.

"Take the wheel, Jim. I'll kill this damn bird!" Larry shouts as he leaps to pull the bird down by its webbed foot. Rising until it's just out of Larry's reach, another yellow-green splat lands on his arm. "Damnation! I'll get you, blasted slob!"

Larry jumps again and the bird squawks *Quack-Queek*.

Managing to grab one foot, feathers fly about Larry's face. Strong wings slap at his face. Jim laughs at the awkward ballet being played in front of him. "I've got you! I'll rip your damned wings off," Larry shouts.

Renewing its efforts, the bird twists and gets loose.

"Come finish the fight, you slob," Larry rants. The bird flies overhead, sending another yellow-green gift to him. "I'll kill you! I'll kill you!" Larry's rage is so overpowering he can hardly talk.

Doubling over with laughter, Jim sputters, "This is great! I've never seen anything funnier!"

"Just hold the wheel steady while I kill this crapper!" Larry grabs a bucket and throws it up at the duck that raises just enough to stay out of reach. The bucket falls back, jams over Larry's head until its handle clanks neatly under his chin. Stumbling over his own feet Larry pulls the bucket off and throws it overboard.

"I'll die if this gets any funnier," Jim says choking with laughter. *Wish Sarah could see this*, he thinks.

"Glad you think it's funny! Gonna kill this bird if it's the last thing I do," Larry vows. "Gimme back the wheel."

The boat swishes in a zig-zag pattern as Larry tries to out maneuver the duck. Suddenly, it changes directions and Larry manages to grab a foot as it alters its course. Holding one bony foot, he avoids the panicked flapping of the duck's wings until he hugs it to his side.

"Got you! Ain't gettin' away this time. Jim, find a rope to tie her down."

As Jim kicks a rope into Larry's reach, the bird twists again and breaks free. Larry lunges in a tackle that misses and ends up holding a bunch of feathers. He lunges a second time and falls overboard with the effort. The duck flies off toward shore.

Grabbing the wheel, Jim asks, "What splashed? Damn, where'd you go, Larry?" Jim keeps the boat circling waiting for his friend to surface. "Gone? Larry, where the hell are you?"

Looking toward shore Jim watches the duck circle one last time while heading back to shore. He hears the familiar, *Quack-Queek*. Jim can't decide if the bird is sounding a victory call or is threatening a return. "What's that? Your grand good-bye?"

Still searching for a sign of Larry, Jim hears a ringing phone. Reaching under a seat, he grabs Larry's cell phone. "Hello?"

Sarah's voice, deep, lusty. "Hello Jim. I've new feathers ready for Friday."

"Sarah? Is that you?"

"Did Larry get the duck I sent? Spent weeks training him just for Larry. You know, I'm great with birds. Larry hated birds. I hated Larry. Uhmmm."

"Larry's gone, Sarah! I think he drowned."

Sarah purrs into the phone. "Come back to shore now, Jim. Be sure to wipe the deck of my new boat before you dock. So sad Larry never learned to swim." Laughing now, "Looking forward to seeing you again, Jim. I'll wait for you at the dock and will bring my longest feathers."

"What a woman!" Jim laughs. "This is the life I've prayed for. I won't think of Larry. I'm on my way."

Steering the boat back to shore, Jim slips on duck feathers smeared with yellow ooze, loses his footing and hits the back of his head on an iron rope tie. Feathers are covered quickly with a dark red stream flowing from his cracked skull.

On the dock, Sarah taps her foot impatiently as she waits for the boat. "I can see it, here it comes! Comin' straight in. Can't wait to rub my honey with new feathers!"

The boat's speed doesn't lessen as it aims at the boat dock. *Too fast*, she thinks. *Why so fast?*

The moment the boat impacts the dock, Sarah is tossed onto the front hull. The last thing she sees is an explosion of body parts mixed with flying duck feathers held together with bloodied mud.

The last thing she hears is: *Quack-Queek.*

About the author:

A graduate of Florida Atlantic University at age sixty-four, Denise is honored by being selected as a finalist in Scribes Valley's 2009 contest. She creates short-stories, children's stories and poetry, and has been published in The Lutheran Digest. A busy grandmother of six, she recently relocated to Atlanta, where she enjoys Southern hospitality. Denise has enjoyed writing fiction for the past twenty years and 'lives to imagine' her work published.

THE TRAIN
©2010 by Kathleen Ratcliffe

"Roundtrip, Center City, please." The attractive fortyish brunette pushed her money through the slot in the thick glass, glancing around at the open newspapers to see if anyone looked up. Not one. Good, she hadn't disturbed a soul. Taking her ticket, she slipped quietly through the station door to the platform. As usual she was one of the first to arrive. Looking at the ground to avoid accidental eye contact she dodged the other pairs of feet and took her place near the tracks.

Mondays! Ugh! They ought to be outlawed in all fifty states and Canada. She hated Mondays all the way to Sunday night. Without fail she allowed her abhorrence of Mondays to ruin her Sundays. This Monday was dreary and wet. All Mondays were dreary. It always rained here, never failed especially on Mondays. How apropos!

Through the heavy mist she stared at the track littered with cigarette butts and crushed plastic bottles. Strange, while it was never cleaned it didn't seem to get any worse.

How well this drab station lent itself to the mood of the early travelers. The hours before dawn were typically quite damp. Dew clung to the colorless pillars of the ancient station. Hovering over the grass was a gray cloud ashamed by its fall from the heavens. Dim lighting, whether intentional or from disrepair, added to the dismal climate.

Several people had arrived. Two were conversing in daring

defiance of the mandated silence. This crime was even worse on the first workday of the lengthy week. What was the matter with them? Did they not know that speech was prohibited at this ungodly hour? Rolling her eyes, she quickly put earphones in to block this bit of human contact. Though not directly involved in the prattle, she found it extremely offensive. She pulled her bulky sweater even tighter to stave off the morning chill.

Standing in this wanton atmosphere she wondered how it was that she was forced to depart for her job so unbelievably early. Not a morning person, she often stated that anything prior to six o'clock should only be p.m. This recurring thought was interrupted by the screeching train whistle.

Coming to a stop right in front of her, the conductors alighted loudly, hawking the destination of the train as if the travelers were ignorant to the route. It only went as far as Center City. The passengers entered the train, claiming their normal seats. She always sat midway down on the right-hand side next to the window.

Beginning the journey alone, invariably solitude was disturbed in three or four stops almost always by a person of quite generous stature. Needless to say, they were always the chatty sort. Why they managed to seek her out was puzzling. She was quite slim and fit but no one would see this. Always draped in the most colossal wraps, she remained hidden from view. Although attractive, her expression shouted "Don't bother me!" Despite her air of isolation some friendly soul always found her during her commute. Whoever it was generally seemed to be of great stature and, of course, cheerful in their discovery of the roomy empty seat next to her.

As today's traveler plopped down next to her with a thud, she gave the largest sigh she could muster given that her breathing room was now greatly depleted. The newcomer made some unsolicited comment on—what else—the weather. She scowled at the remark. Trying again only to be rebuffed, the person retreated to a book. They rode silently to the same Center City stop.

Following the exodus of workers, she trekked on to her building. By rote, she appeared in her office and at her desk, though unable to recall the walk from the train. Everything in her life was automatic: no thought, no change, no challenge.

The day continued in much the same fashion. The same people said the same things, cracked the same jokes, and wore the same expressions. Lack of windows gave each day an identical feeling no matter the day, no matter the season. A nuclear holocaust could occur between the hours of seven a.m. and four in the afternoon and the occupants of the work place would be none the wiser.

Repetition was depressing. Many years ago, she had tried to break the monotony by attempting some diversions. She'd tried dressing more fashionably, driving in on occasion, even dining in town. This was huge as she detested dining alone. While her actions cheered her for the short term, redundancy won out, squashing what little progress she had achieved.

Work did nothing to soothe her. After many years in the same position she found this job dull. This had not always been the case. Initially, she worked with great zeal. Her enthusiasms lead her to formulate improvements to yield more efficiency. On more than one occasion she had come up with fantastic ideas, at least to her estimation. But suggestions on different enhancements were greeted with "But this is how we've always done it." So often was she rebuffed that she finally surrendered to the company way, battling no more.

Consoling herself, she decided this non-demanding job gave her more freedom. Passing up promotions to management or supervisory levels meant not staying late and no deadlines to meet. Not that she did anything with that extra time but it was there none the less. Besides, her humdrum job complimented her lackluster life. There was nothing in it to give her any spark. There was nothing to interrupt all the necessary tasks. Weekends were spent alone doing wash, cleaning and straightening. The thought of making changes to her living quarters never entered her head. The sparsely decorated dwelling was in exactly the same order as it had been thirteen years ago.

Her logic was that while she could afford a house, the apartment gave her more options. Leases were year to year, no yard to tend; all maintenance was the landlord's responsibility. Lack of change was easily rationalized. You can't paint or alter an apartment. Why redecorate if one day you might move? Not that there was a remote prospect of that. And so she was defeated, not so much in her own mind, but perhaps because of it. In truth she had taken chances before, a good many. But they always resulted in disappointment, sometimes severe. No need to keep setting yourself up for a letdown.

Eight long hours concluded. Reversing the path she had taken that morning, she arrived at her sanctuary. Today she was treated to the luxury of riding without a seat companion for the entire trip. This was a rare treat. No reading today, no working, she sat in the middle of the bench seat staring at nothing, just nothing. As her station was announced she sprung up to exit, nearly knocking a well-dressed man into the next seat. Quickly they mumbled apologies and, heads down, made their way forward. For some unknown reason this exchange piqued her interest. Waiting for the train to stop, she surveyed the man before her.

Impeccably dressed in a rich navy wool coat, he carried a burgundy leather brief case. The gloves he wore matched the case so well she assumed they were cut from the same hide. The gray wool "Jeff cap" he wore suited him. So well-groomed was he that she could not discern so much as one speck on his garb.

Though not a pretty man, he had a face that instilled confidence. He bore a look of credibility and experience. A businessman, or perhaps a lawyer, must be his line. She imagined his eloquence while a jury listened to his delivery, their hands clutched near their chest in admiration. She watched the man get into his car, start it up, wait a minute and drive off. Continuing to sit in her car for a few minutes before starting the engine, she felt unable to move. Usually she zipped out of the parking lot. Tonight for some reason, she waited a few more minutes before starting her short ride.

The next morning, it was the same thing all over again, but this time when she turned away from the ticket counter, she paused slightly and looked at that same man she had run into last evening. He must have felt her eyes on him. He peeked up ever so slightly. Was it at her? Quickly she looked away and went out to the platform.

Throughout the long day she found herself thinking of the momentary exchange between herself and that well attired man. Something happened between them ever so briefly last night. Then there it was again this morning. He looked at her, she was certain. Without realizing it, this small contact brightened her dull life. Silly, yet she couldn't wait for the ride home. He must be there every day, yet she'd not seen him. No surprise as she never looked at any of the other commuters.

Few people spoke to each other, the ones that did congregated in their own little section. She never gave them much notice. It wasn't like her to join in or even look their way. This time alone was indispensable before and after her incredibly tedious job. However, if he spoke to her how nice that would be. They wouldn't have to share a ride in. Not yet anyway.

Sitting in her customary seat, she attempted to read. Noticing that the words were too recognizable, she became aware that she'd re-read the same page several times. As her station neared, she considered a casual look around but refrained. She stood up slowly as the train closed in on her destination. Timidly she scouted the car of the train in search of that gentleman. He was there. He was getting himself together to depart. She took a deep breath and remained at her seat, allowing other passengers to exit. He started up the aisle, staggering as the train swerved along the tracks. She glanced up as he went past but the look was not returned. Sadly she stepped out behind him. Waiting for the others to disembark, he turned ever so slightly toward her. Was that a smile or had she imagined it? The skin on the back of her neck felt prickly. Both of her ears burned. Her mind in overdrive, she thought perhaps he would wait for her in the parking lot. Casually he would make some small comment that would cause them both to laugh, then he would introduce himself and...but stop, she told herself as she watched him walk to his car, get in, start it up, wait for a minute and drive off.

"So now, instead of the same old thing over and over, it will be the same old thing over and over. Plus, I will be watching him and day dreaming like a pubescent prude with no real life so one must be fabricated. And it's not even a very interesting creation!" She shook her head as she got into her car and drove home. How had it come to this? How was it that her little life was so dull that she had to live for a *tête-à-tête* that would never be? In the shadowy light of her bedroom she sat at her dressing table. Glancing only slightly at her vision, she scolded herself for this foolishness.

Thinking of escaping her idiocy through work, she nixed this idea at once. Work was a poor diversion. Not only was the triteness of the job distressing, she had no cronies to distract her. She felt out of place among her co-workers. The office had evolved over time. While she passed up promotions, others did not. Over the years her colleagues had either moved up the ladder or taken jobs closer to home. Some even had the nerve to work less hours. While never forming liaisons with these people, she'd been used to them. Their lives were very similar to hers, but she'd never taken the time to discover this fact. Now a younger set graced the workplace. Their nonchalance bothered her. They worried about nothing other than esthetics and fun. Soothing herself, she thought of their dismay when they discovered the tedium that was life.

Having done nothing to attract these people as comrades, the new workers shied away from her. It was easy to read the "stay away from me" look she glared. Their world was foreign to her. There was no reason to show any interest in their escapades. Besides, they didn't like her. They made snide comments that hurt her. She overheard the whispers, "Maybe if she'd get it once a year she'd be human."

Behind her back they referred to her as "Robot," a reference to her conformity to habit. While she insisted these things did not affect her, she had winced when she overheard them. In fact, this encounter on the train was more of a distraction from work than vice versa. Like it or not she thought of it all the more.

The next several excursions to her job were replays of that event. She swore that man looked at her, and then she swore he did not. As days wore on she began to concoct possible scenarios. She would bump into him. They would mumble apologies and dash off to their cars. Suddenly, he would stop dead, come over to her and confess that he had always wanted to speak to her, perhaps get to know her. Here fate had presented him with the opportunity and he was about to let it slip away. They would talk on until one of them noticed that it was getting dark. He would ask for her phone number, she'd give it. By the time she got home the phone would be ringing--him, of course. They'd talk on and on, etc. The next day, the train station would be ablaze with lights. A golden sun would be edging up to greet the station. She'd buy her ticket, look back to see if he was looking back only to find him at her side. Well, she liked that one.

Then there was the one where she was sitting by the window when suddenly, she felt someone sit next to her. To her amazement, it was him. She tried to act nonchalant, reading her book. He took out his newspaper and began to peruse the headlines. They sat in silence for several minutes when he hit the paper with his hand, making a remark which caused her to laugh. Conversation ensued leading them to discover how many things they had in common. Similar views, tastes and experiences led them to the conclusion that they absolutely needed to spend an evening together very soon...say this weekend. They continued a lighthearted discussion of events for the rest of their trip. Then, to their amazement, they would discover they shared the same Center City stop. More surprise when they found they were walking in the same direction. But the biggest and best revelation came when they found they worked in the same building. After all this time they never knew! Yes, this one was good as well.

Daydreams were unfamiliar invaders of her normal thoughts. So regimented was her thinking that she never allowed herself any fantasies. This was far too frivolous, much like the musing of her juvenile coworkers. In the past she believed that dreaming would lead to false hopes which would not be good for her morale. Had she examined herself further she would have seen that her morale was already quite low, having been that way for some time. Without her comprehension, this little production had lifted her from the drone of her usual existence.

This thing had become so tangible she could almost touch it. How could anything be so concrete and ethereal at once? Imagined conversations gave way to intimacy. She thought of his touch, the feel of his hand on her shoulder, the warmth of his breath on her cheek. Day after day she found herself on the wrong side of the snow globe. How could she make her way inside?

Suddenly she realized someone was looking at her. Opening her eyes wide she jumped before realizing that it was only her reflection in the window. How old she looked. Her face had a mean expression. Making a face at herself she quickly looked away. A scan of the area to see if anyone noticed that little drama convinced her that there were no witnesses. She sighed with relief.

Who are you kidding? she thought. *You're like a ridiculous love-starved school girl romanticizing about something that will never be. There's no wedding ring but there may still be someone in his life.* She closed her eyes again and envisioned him opening a picket gate, walking up a flagstone walkway to a charming white house with a red door. As he drew nearer, the door swung open and out came a perfect wife followed by perfect children, bright-eyed and beaming at seeing father was home. The group hug and happy banter would continue as they retired happily into their abode, red door closing them off from the world. *That's probably closer to the truth*, she resigned.

Friday morning came at last. The week was coming to a close. Everyone seemed chipper this morning, the elevated mood evidenced by chatter which broke the a.m. silence. She looked over to where the well-dressed man was sitting and discovered he was engaged in conversation with one of the other men. They were both rather lively, smiling at each other's comments. Then there it was. He looked right at her. There was no mistaking it, he did look at her. The prickly feeling on her neck started up. Her throat was bone dry. The water fountain was five paces away but almost right next to where the men were speaking. What if she took a sip, swallowed wrong and spit all over them? What if she started to choke and one of them had to perform the Heimlich maneuver? She would die a thousand deaths. But if she didn't have a sip of water she'd suffocate. They'd have to stop to get her on an ambulance and the whole train of people would be furious with her.

Purposefully she sat down in the station, feigning a search through her bag for a necessary item. The train whistle sounded, causing the few in the station to go out to the platform. Once the two men had exited, she quickly got to the water fountain and, as predicted, dribbled half of her intake onto her dress. Pulling her thick cardigan closed to cover the stain she joined the others as the train arrived.

As she waited her turn to board, the man in front of her stepped aside to let her pass. It was him. How could she not have noticed him right in front of her? *Oh, my heavens!"* He was going to let her choose a seat so he could sit next to her. It was actually happening as she pictured. She felt shaky. *Please don't let the knees buckle on the way down the aisle.* As quick as possible, she found her seat, moving in so he could join her. But he was no longer behind. *Where the hell did he go?* Craning to see up the aisle, she found the top of his head several rows away. Of course, he was sitting with the man from the station. But why did he let her ahead? Maybe he was going to sit with her but his purpose was disturbed by this interloper. Perhaps he was also disappointed. No matter. She'd see him on the way home. It would work out. It had to work out.

But it was not to be. Her gentleman was nowhere to be seen. Now she had all weekend, two long days, forty-eight hours of eternity, to plot, to plan to hope, and to obsess. Indeed, it was the longest weekend she could recall. For once the time off was unwelcome.

Preparing for bed that Friday night, she sat at her dressing table examining her reflection. Not her usual practice of discreetly peering at herself, she looked closely at her face for the first time in many years. The person looking back actually astonished her. The smooth chestnut tresses were in splendid condition. Styled simply, neither trendy nor dated, they were really pretty. A clear complexion and few facial lines were the result of minimal sun exposure as well as good genes. Years of ballet resulted in perfect posture. She grinned at herself, and then laughed as her facial muscles ached from minimal use.

Drinking in her image, her smile grew. Speaking aloud to the mirror, she scolded, "Mary Jean, look at you! Why you're not bad. Not bad at all. Many women your age don't look nearly as good. You've sold yourself short." Smiling again she felt encouraged.

The rest of the weekend soared by as always, but this time she spent it differently. She took several long walks in the nearby park, enjoying the magnificent weather. Spring had chased away the starkness of winter. Flowers bloomed, animals scurried about, all contributing to her lofty spirits. Everything looked wonderful and new.

Maintaining her optimism all weekend, by Sunday night she was convinced that this opportunity must be snatched. Carefully considering all options, she devised a plan. Monday morning was not the time to pounce, she decided. Most people were fairly unapproachable until Wednesday. More than ever she knew she must be patient. To ignite interest, she decided that she must make herself more alluring. In order to accomplish this she had to create desire in case it was not already a factor. By taking other transportation to work she hoped he would notice her absence. The man would be puzzled, which would cause him to wonder about her, perhaps yearn. This would pave the way for part two of her plan—she would have to approach him. Missing her might even drive *him* to make the initial move. That would be optimum, but she would not count on this possibility.

More than ready for the start of a new week she greeted Monday with anticipation. This would be her week. Sticking with her plan she drove to work knowing that all too soon her goal would come to fruition.

Finally, the day was here. She was ready for work in record time. Inspecting herself before leaving, she approved of her appearance. She looked stunning. Grabbing her bag and slipping on her oversized sweater she headed for the door. The cumbersome garb was almost on before she tore it off, flinging it on the sofa. Purposely she left late, timing it so she would just make the train. Looking through the passengers she saw him studying the area. Was it for her? After two days of absence—two and a half if he didn't see her this morning—he would be primed by this evening.

The day passed slowly. Every hour seemed like two. At last it was time to leave for the train. Her heart was pounding in her ears as she found her seat. Trying to calm herself, she awaited his arrival. Relief set in once he appeared. Three rows away from her, she watched the back of his head throughout the journey. Their stop was announced. He rose, as did she. Before she could get to the aisle, an elderly woman stepped between them. The old woman moved slowly, burdened with a huge bag. The man maintained his usual pace.

How could this be happening? It was certainly not in the plan.

As she trudged down the steep train steps to the platform, the old lady tripped. Mary Jean and the conductor quickly grabbed the woman to prevent her from toppling to the ground. Unfortunately, her bag had flown out of her arms, spilling its entire contents all over the wooden walkway. With great reluctance Mary Jean helped gather the items. Brushing off the words of gratitude she raced to the parking lot hoping her chance was not gone.

Thank goodness! There he was walking just ahead. Where was his car? There was still time to catch him. Quickening her pace she continued the pursuit. Now there was nothing more to stand in the way.

This is it!

She had almost reached him when she saw that he had stopped and *Oh No!* he was getting into the passenger side of some other car. There was a woman in the driver's seat!

I knew it! she thought. *No ring, but that doesn't mean anything. I should have known he'd be married. Everyone is. I always end up disappointed. It never fails.* Forlorn, she got in to her car and sat for a moment before starting the engine.

Had she looked over, she would have seen him gazing back at her, just as he had so many times before. "She's lovely," the woman in the driver's seat said. "I thought I saw her looking over at you."

"You must need glasses," he mumbled, then smiled the slightest of smiles. "Thanks for picking me up."

The woman patted his hand. "Think nothing of it. That's what sisters are for."

About the author:

Kathleen Ratcliffe is a registered nurse whose career is divided between working clinically in a cardiac catherization laboratory and providing education to medical professionals all over the United States. Employed by a small company in Pennsylvania, her job involves composing educational material and instruction of the clinical aspects of invasive cardiology.

During the past fifteen years she became a single parent, studied to become a registered nurse and raised two children with the help of her wonderful mother. She then pursued a bachelor _ s degree while working to support her family. After years of writing papers and presentations related to nursing, she has been afforded the time to go back to writing fiction. Several stories are complete and others are in progress.

As sports editor for her high school paper, she attended a journalism seminar for high school editors at the Catholic University in Washington D.C. It was there where her fervor for writing expanded.

The proud mother of two children, her son is a PhD candidate in anthropology at Temple University. Her daughter is a student at Montgomery County Community College.

Besides writing, Kathleen's interests include running, cycling and yoga. Her fiancé, who is also a registered nurse, introduced her to the world of triathlon several years ago. Helping her conquer her fear of open water swimming, he made her realize that anything is possible if you try.

THE OTHER SIDE
©2010 by Andrew Lu

The Black Gate lay asunder, a heap of twisted, smoking iron. The Guardians were felled, their steaming corpses smouldering in their own foul blood. The Khahasar, the Black Legion, were decimated and scattered, helpless against the foe. Their blood painted the walls and ran down the steps of the Citadel. Even the Horrors, chained and bound for centuries, had been loosed, a desperate measure; they, too, were destroyed, lying like mountains of flesh in the courtyards, their very scent carrying death to any mortal creature. The last line of defense, the lich-lords, the Wraiths, the most powerful servants of the dark master—even they were now falling before the enemy, writhing in unspeakable agony as they dissipated into black dust on the ebon stones of the Hall of Endings.

Now, there was but one left, but he was the greatest of all. The Black Lord, Father of Night, Eater of Souls, Devourer of Worlds—Azharis. The Dark God. He sat on his throne of skulls and waited, his eyes fixed on the darkened bronze of the doors to his chamber. With one final wail, the last of the lich-lords fell. There was silence.

Azharis waited. His blood-red eyes never left the door.

A moment later, the great bronze doors shuddered under a mighty blow, ringing sonorously like a giant gong. Infinitesimally tiny, black stone flakes dislodged themselves from the ceiling and lazily drifted down. The chamber doors shuddered once more and cracks spidered up the walls. The flames of the braziers wavered. Still Azharis sat upon his throne, unmoving.

The postern rang a third time. This time they burst asunder and into the throne room, into the Last Chamber, burst the enemy.

He was a huge man, positively massive, clad head to toe in brilliant, shining armor, silver as the stars. His sword glowed with the light of ten suns, and his shield with the light of ten moons. His footsteps rang like silver bells as he advanced slowly into the throne room of the Dark God.

Here at last was the Hero. The Paladin. The Champion. The Vanquisher of Evil. He was a confident beacon of power and purity, shining in the shadows of the Black Lord's kingdom.

"At last," said the Hero. "At last it has come to this. At last goodness stands in the heart of the Citadel, and Evil trembles before the Light." He raised his sword and pointed it at the hulking shadow on the throne. "Here, it will be finished. This is the final battle. This is the end. Prepare yourself, ye demon!"

Azharis sighed. There was silence for a moment.

"Have you nothing to say, Shadowking?" demanded the Hero, waving his holy sword imperiously.

"What? No, not really," said the Dark God. "I was just wondering if you were done."

The Hero blinked. His face was hidden behind the arcane silvery metal of his helm, but Azharis could still tell. He was a god, after all; he knew these things. Quickly, though, the Hero regained his composure.

"No, fiend," said he, stepping forward. "It is you who is done. Your reign will finally be ended. The people of this world will be free of your scourge forever."

Shaking his head, Azharis folded his black, clawed hands together. "It's always this way with you people. Never any consideration. Never any sympathy. And they call *me* the nasty one."

The Hero paused. This wasn't how it was supposed to go.

"It's always the same," the Dark God continued, waving his

talons sadly. "You rascals...always coming in here, wrecking the place, killing minions left and right, flinging holy fire this way and holy water that way and smashing all my nice pottery. You know, you're supposed to come right up to the top of the big tower in the middle. Instead, you go around, laying waste. There's really no need."

The Hero gaped but recovered momentarily. "You...you...but surely, you see...the hellish works of evil must be purged from the land. Your vile creations must be destroyed."

Azharis rolled his eyes. "I've heard it all before. I don't suppose anyone told you how this all works?"

"Well, not as such, no," said the Hero. "I...I was reasonably certain that I would come in here, vanquish your minions, destroy your dark legacy, and then engage you in a climactic, mortal duel for the fate of the world."

"And then what?" Azharis asked expectantly.

"I...you..." the Hero stammered. "Well, you'd be, er, vanquished, of course, and there would be peace and prosperity and happiness for centuries to come. I'd win the hand of the Princess, become a prince and eventually the King...the standard denouement really..."

The Dark God stared at him. The Hero stared back. He wasn't quite sure what to do with his sword. He had been keeping it pointed at the hellion but he thought he detected the faint beginnings of an arm cramp. After quite some deliberation, he warily lowered the tip to the ground.

"What?" the Hero said finally. "That's how it goes."

"Is it?" said Azharis. "I say, do I look vanquished to you?"

"Er...no. You look rather, ah, robust," the Hero said. "For an evil doer," he added hastily.

"Well, do you think you're the first Hero to come up here and start waving your sword at me and talking about the end and final battles and such?"

"Of course not!" the Hero exclaimed. This he knew. "There was Victor the Great, and Lothar the Holy, and Samar the White, and…that big fellow with the hammer, what was his name…"

"Gabriel?"

"Yes!" cried the Hero. "Yes, Gabriel, that's the one."

"So, you see my point, then."

The Hero looked at the Dark God blankly.

"I'm, ah, not vanquished," Azharis said helpfully. "So, these things, these 'final battles,' they don't seem to involve a whole lot of vanquishing, do they?"

"No, I suppose not," mused the Hero. "But, you *were* defeated! And, your power reduced, you were driven into exile, never to appear again for centuries!"

"Yes, you see, that's what I'm talking ab—"

"Then I shall defeat you, and the world shall be safe until such time as you reappear!" the Hero shouted, waving his sword with great conviction.

The Dark God rubbed his temple with one clawed hand and did his best to ignore the rivulets of blood beginning to run down his face. "They never seem to tell anyone how this works," he muttered. "Might as well just give a holy sword to a moose and call him the Hero."

"No, not moose, they're bull horns," said the Hero.

"What?"

"The horns." The Hero pointed to his shining helmet. "They're bull horns, from a holy white bull on the Isle of Exelsus."

"That's, um, very nice," said Azharis. "Now, you see, here's how this is going to work."

"How what is going to work?"

"This whole, you know, final battle thing."

"Oh."

"You're going to stick me with that sword, that nice one there in your hand, and I'm going to say something along the lines of 'Oh no, I am vanquished, but I shall return, you haven't seen the last of me,' etc. And then I'm going to pull that lever, over there, see, the big red one, yes, that's the one, no, don't touch it, you idiot. There's a good boy. I'm going to pull that one, and that will set off the self-destruction mechanism for the Citadel. Everything will start to collapse. You will make a daring escape, leaping from falling stone to falling stone, swinging from parapet to parapet, you know how it goes. It'll be very dramatic, good story for the grandchildren. Meanwhile, I get to retire for a few centuries, maybe catch up on my reading, while you live out your nice long life as a Hero, perhaps saving cats from trees and pulling old people out of burning houses and the like. When the time comes, I'll just throw together a new Citadel at some extreme point of the map, fix up some new minions, and the whole thing will start up again. By then, of course, you'll be dead, and no doubt some other young zealous fool, perhaps a distant descendant of yours, will be a part of an ancient prophecy or something, and he'll get your sword and proceed to "vanquish" me all over again. Got it?"

The Hero stared.

Azharis sighed again. "Look, sorry for going off on you like that. I'm just so tired of this whole tired shtick. Just give me a little poke, and I'll pull the lever, and you run like hell. Easy as pie."

"It seems like you get off rather easy, though," said the Hero. "I mean, you're all evil and nasty and destructive and everything, and you just get poked once, and then you're off to the beaches for a relaxing vacation reading Satre? Hardly seems fair. Seems there's no, what do you call it, justice. Doesn't seem fair at all."

"No justice?" the Dark God asked incredulously. "No justice? You speak to me of what is fair? *I'm* the one who has to sit here, holed up in this bloody dark tower for years on end, telling slackjawed troglodyte minions what to do, tying their shoes for them, organizing their raids, dealing with idiots like you who can't even deliver a one-liner properly, while all the other gods get to prance around half-naked, drinking wine and schmoozing with easy mortal women, and you say there's no justice?"

"I—"

"Do you have any idea how difficult it is to be evil all the time? Really? Do you? I have to be a right bastard to everyone, forever! It's quite wearing! Sometimes, I just want to feed a rabbit some strawberries or something, but I can't, because I'm the Dark God! I'm the Devourer of Worlds! Do you know how much bloody pressure there is? Do you know how depressing it is to wear all black, all the time, for three thousand years? DO YOU HAVE ANY IDEA WHAT IT FEELS LIKE TO HAVE YOUR HAIR PERMANENTLY ON FIRE?"

"You—"

"They told me it would be a revolving schedule. You know, one millennium I get to be evil, the next, it's someone else, and I get to be a...a love god, or a wine god or something. Something fun, you know? I even volunteered to be the first Dark God. I thought it would be a lark. Let me tell you, it's not. It's not fun at all anymore. I can't even enjoy the simple pleasure of watching peasants run screaming these days."

"But—"

"And you're all so ungrateful, you self-righteous buffoons. I do this for you—*for you*—present a big, juicy common foe, a terrifying dark presence that mankind can unite against, who just happens to be conveniently defeated at all the right times. I do this, and what do I get? 'Your dark reign is at an end! Your vile works must be destroyed!' No appreciation at all! None!" After a few moments of indignant glaring, Azharis lapsed into sullen silence.

The Hero stood awkwardly on the steps before the throne of skulls. "So...I, er, just poke you with the sword, then?" he asked quietly. "There's no battle?"

"What? No, there's no battle. I'm a god, you ninny. I could turn you into a booger before you could fumble a one-liner."

"Oh."

"Well, all right then, let's get on with it. I got a little carried away there, but really, it's not so bad. I get a good few centuries of retirement." Azharis stood up, towering a dozen feet above the Hero. "Go on, poke away. It's really just a formality, but it's tradition, you know."

"Oh. Yes," said the Hero. He drew back the holy sword, then paused.

"What is it now?"

"Um...well..." the Hero said uncertainly. "I...well, I, for one, would like to say, um, thank you."

Azharis stared. "Really?"

"Oh, yes," the Hero said. "You're...you're doing a bang-up job, I must say."

"You think so?"

"Oh, definitely, definitely. Evil as they come. Had me fooled completely. Hasn't even been a real war between the kingdoms for almost a thousand years."

Azharis smiled, his fangs glowing pleasantly in the light of the glowing Hero below him. "Well, that's very kind of you. That makes me feel much better, really. I must say, you make a rather fine Hero yourself."

"Oh, you're too kind."

"No, really, you dispatched those orcs with ineffable style. And you butchered the lich-lords quite handily. Usually they're a bit of trouble. They even killed one poor chap a few centuries ago, threw the whole schedule off."

"Oh my."

"Yes, it was quite the conundrum."

"Well, thank you."

"Not at all."

They stood in awkward yet affable silence for a moment.

"I suppose we should get on with it," said the Dark God.

"Indeed."

"It was nice meeting you," said Azharis, placing a clawed hand on the red lever.

"The pleasure was all mine," said the Hero. And then, he poked the Dark God lightly on the chest with the holy sword.

And then, with a mighty blow, the Hero vanquished the Dark God, who screamed in rage, and promised to return for vengeance on this world once more, before vanishing into the darkness from whence he came. No longer supported by its master's dark power, the Citadel began to collapse, and the Hero made a daring and narrow escape before the dark realm was drawn back into the abyss. And the Hero lived happily ever after with his beautiful princess bride and the adoration of his subjects, and he left as his legacy the holy armor and sword, so that when the Dark God returns again, there will be another Hero to face him and defeat him and keep the world safe once more.

Or something like that.

About the author:

Andrew Lu is a high school senior studying (and living) at Stevenson, a boarding school in Pebble Beach, CA. This story will be his first appearance in an anthology so he is still unused to talking about himself in the third person. His favorite genres are science fiction and fantasy, with a healthy dose of humor, a combination that can be seen in his story 'The Other Side.' Though he is proud of his accomplishments so far (he thanks his teachers, family, and friends), he recognizes how much he can still improve.

THE MIGHTY BLUE
©2010 by Brian James

As I lie in my hospital bed, I recall the memory of my grandfather the last time I saw him lying in a similar position hooked to pumps and monitors. A much younger man at the time, I remember walking into the room and seeing his head roll across the pillow to face me. His eyes were barely opened. In their cavernous sockets laid thin slices of clear Caribbean water, as if cut right from the sea and shrouded by his feral brow. He had appeared much older than I ever remembered him being, but those sparkling eyes still tried to light the world with the last flicker of flame left inside.

We talked.

His voice was soft, muffled behind the plastic mask designed to keep the oxygen flowing to him, although he heaved air into his lungs with a whistling squeal, like he was trying to suck dry sand from mud. Machines hummed and beeped in the background. The stiff scent of antiseptics mixed with bad hospital food stung my nose, an aroma I still haven't gotten used to. I'd hoped he couldn't smell the concoction from behind that mask. It alone would have been enough to do him in.

I told him how much I loved him and he replied with a kind, "I love you too, son," like I was his son and not his grandson. I thanked him for being such an important part of my life, for helping to shape me into the man I had become. He was silent for a moment and then evoked a memory of a time when I was just a boy, some twenty years earlier. It was a memory I had nearly forgotten. As he rambled between strained breaths about it, a warm sensation came over me, like someone had thrown one of my grandmother's hand-sewn quilts over my shoulders. He finished the thought by saying, "We'll have to do that again someday."

In lieu of a response I smiled, knowing that was not going to happen. He had to know that too, yet he said it anyway. Empty promises were never one of those conversational consignments my grandfather invested in, and he had to know what was coming, so I found it peculiar that he chose those to be his final words.

He returned a smile to me and closed his eyes. Seconds later, the monitor sounded an alarm, and it reminded me of a toy fire truck he'd given me for my eighth birthday.

That seems like several lifetimes ago now.

Nurses rushed past me. I remained, staring, his smile still pasted on his weathered face. One of the nurses politely excused me from the room. She shut me off from the chaos—the scurrying about, checking for vitals, the injections of life-saving serums. I knew it was pointless.

He had already left.

As I stood alone in the hall on that dreadful day, I realized that my grandfather had used his last breath to teach me one final life lesson, a lesson that a teacher could only conduct once in his life and one that could only be taught at that very moment. I felt special because of that...saddened, but special. To me, Pop-Pop was more than just a grandfather; he was my friend, my mentor. He had been retired for as long as I'd known him, and he'd taken on the task of making me his pupil since my father had worked too many hours and gotten home way too late to spend much quality time with me growing up.

Pop-Pop was a slight man, maybe 5 feet 6 inches and 160 pounds, with thinning grey hair. His piercing blue eyes possessed a lifetime of knowledge, relentless determination, and a hint of mystery. Just beyond them—those worlds of wisdom—lingered things he'd kept to himself; things I had always wondered about and knew he wanted to tell me, but never did.

During his final minutes, I expected his long-held secrets to be revealed. He remained conscious and logical and insanely calm given the circumstances. Maybe it was because of that fond memory he'd brought back from the far reaches of his brain. I wondered if he would have thought of that moment if another member of the family had arrived before me. It was a strange and magical feeling knowing that a recollection of us together was the last thought to go through his head, my face the last he'd ever see, and our conversation the last he'd ever take part in. I felt a transition of sorts during the exchange of smiles, like he'd passed something along to me. But I was too distressed and still too young to uncover its meaning. For as slowly as time had passed for me growing to become a man, the same time had rushed along and taken its toll on him, finally catching up and then running out.

My grandfather, Pop-Pop, had died.

Although I had felt as if no good could come in this life without him there, time still clicked by. Months turned to years and years turned to decades. I have closed in on the age he was when he passed, and now ponder what he'd meant with his final words, "We'll have to do that again someday." As monitors beep next to my bed, I recall the memory he'd conjured up during those last moments.

It was from a time when I was ten years old. We had gone fishing, a rare occurrence; my grandfather, my father, and me together out on the open ocean, the two grown men dutifully passing along generations of experience and knowledge to the youngest of their bloodline. We were going for bluefish and had had a successful day already when Pop-Pop hooked the big one.

Notorious fighters, bluefish are relatively small in comparison to other game fish, usually eight to twelve pounds in size. But they have a relentless will to live. They never give up. Many fish tire after a long battle on the end of a line, and the final haul is just reeling in dead weight. But with bluefish, you have to fight them all the way to the deck—and to the death.

His pole bent over the rail as the line whizzed from the reel. The monster fish took the bait and headed for deeper water. Pop-Pop removed the pole from the metal cylinder that held it in place and almost lost the handle. His belly pressed against the painted rail and his entire upper body leaned over it, like a pirate's plank hovering above the sloshing ocean.

He managed to hang on and pulled back to gain leverage on the thing that continued to steal the heavy-gauged line deeper into the sea. As ferocious as they are, none of us had ever seen a blue pull as hard as this one did and my father concluded that it had to be something bigger.

I stood in awe of my mighty granddad. His forearms bore straining tendons. His knuckles turned white as he started to reel in what seemed like a half a mile of line that the fish had stolen. His pole bent further, stretching even more toward the water.

Then we heard a crack.

Pop-Pop stepped back from the rail, still cranking out one hard fought turn after another on the reel. But his rod had snapped and the thin spindly end began to slide down the line toward the ocean. He now had no leverage to fight the fish, rendering the reel useless. Pop-Pop told me to give him my sweatshirt. I didn't realize why he was asking for that at a moment like this, but I complied nonetheless. I pulled it over my head. He told me to wrap it around his forearm and tie the arms of it in a knot at his wrist.

I did.

Pop-Pop then dropped the reel to the deck and began wrapping line around the sweatshirt on his forearm.

My father laughed and said, "Dad, just let it go. It's got you beat."

I swear I saw a blue flame shoot from Pop-Pop's eyes.

He rolled his arm over and stepped back from the rail, then wrapped more of the taut line around the sweatshirt. He continued this for over an hour, back and forth, sweat pouring from his forehead. His hands bled as the line sliced through his wrinkled skin. His arm became this tangled spool of used barbed wire, dripping with a mixture of seawater and blood. My sweatshirt was ruined, but it was worth the price to witness this magnificent feat.

We saw the splash as the fish broke the water's surface for the first time, just twenty or so feet from the boat.

I yelled, "Whoa!"

It was a blue all right, and it was huge—five times the size of any we had caught that day. Its tail clapped the water and, holding true to form, the fish dove for the bottom again. Pop-Pop put his foot against the rail to keep from being pulled in after it. My father grabbed him around the waist to assure that didn't happen.

Pop-Pop wrapped more and more line around his arm. The fish came to the surface once again, this time just below us. It began slapping against the side of the boat with frequent thuds. With my father working a gaff, Pop-Pop continued with the line, wrapping it five or six more times around his arm before they were able to heave the fish over the rail.

The creature was as big as me. It thrashed on the deck, trying to find its way back to the water. The mouth gaped open and revealed rows of angled transparent teeth like thousands of clear toothpicks placed at random.

After a few minutes, the fish grew weary. With no obvious escape, it finally settled, seeming to accept its fate. Its red gills rose and fell in silence. Its eye darted back and forth, scanning us, as if to acknowledge its victors. Calmness fell over it. Stoic and beautiful, even during its demise, the blue had represented more than just a good fight. Though it had been beaten, its will was something to be admired. It had fought as hard as it could and its acceptance of the outcome demanded as much respect as its fight. My grandfather smiled and pulled me to him.

Of all the amazing times we had shared, it was this small moment that he chose to remember at the end of his life. We had never spoken of that trip after it ended, and I was surprised to hear him mention it then.

But now...now as I recall his memory, I have also taken his place. The siren of my toy fire truck wails from the monitor next to my bed and only now do I realize what it was Pop-Pop had meant. He had confirmed for me in that one sentence, with his final breath, that I had passed life's tests and everything would be okay. I would be fine without him because all of that time was temporary. He knew we would meet again. Our journey was not over. Many more fishing trips lay ahead of us. This was the secret he had been hiding and waited all his life for that very moment to reveal to me. I now know there is a special place beyond here, somewhere for us to continue our voyage.

The fish seemed to know it.

He saw that.

Now, I do, too.

He's there waiting for me, my granddad—the mighty blue.

About the author:

Brian James is a summa cum laude graduate of a small college in South Carolina. Now residing in Columbia, he started writing only three years ago and his passion for it has exploded. His works tend to focus on the inexplicable interactions between the world we live in and those mysterious realms beyond, where the living have yet to explore. His supernatural horror novel, *D1SORD3R*, was a semi-finalist in the 2007 Amazon.com Breakthrough Novel contest with *Publisher's Weekly* calling it, "a story worth reading." He has also received an award for his short story, "In the Face of a Miracle," from Writer's Digest.

Brian and his wife of seven years are both passionate dog-lovers, having rescued over a dozen so far placing them in loving homes, including three in their own. Brian is in the process of completing his second novel while still producing a wealth of short stories.

THE DAY TRADER
©2010 by Terry Dickinson

He was beginning to feel a cramp in his wrist and his index finger was involuntarily twitching over the computer mouse. Same position too long without moving. He pulled his hand back and put it in his lap as if it belonged to someone else. A cold November wind was driving sleet against the office window. He watched as it melted and sagged down the glass like tears. Cold sweat beaded on his forehead.

He had hardly moved since the stock market had opened at 9:30. Red and green lights flickered as his watch-list on the trading screen gained and lost. The green bar on the right edge of the chart just went red. The stock was now trading below last night's closing price. The Dow Industrials were still in positive territory, but dropping, now up slightly, lower, up, but not as far, now negative.

His finger was twitching again. He didn't remember putting his hand back on the mouse. Before the market opened he had filled out a buy order. The arrow of the mouse was positioned on the SEND ORDER icon. His wrist was cramping. Will it go lower? Is this the time to buy? The market should go up today. Job losses were not as bad as expected. Before the regular trading hours had opened the Dow and Nasdaq futures bounced up on the news. The little cursor arrow reminded him of his younger years when he used to bow hunt, sitting motionless with shallow, silent breaths, waiting for an open shot as a long-awaited deer sniffed its way toward the bait pile. His fingers twitched then, too. A quick glance at the upper right corner of his monitor, it was 10:37:32 AM. Outside it was getting colder and the wind moaned through the spruce tree he had transplanted several years ago. Its needles glistened with frozen sleet.

The mournful sound reminded him of his mother. She sort of hummed, long low tones like a pipe organ with too much bass, when she paced the floor worried. She worried a lot. A single parent carries a lot of responsibility. It's scary. In his mind's eye he could see her as she circled the kitchen nervously humming and rearranging the spices or watering the African Violets that adorned the windowsill. The scene repeated like ritual throughout his childhood. She seldom smiled. Life was serious and filled with unseen dangers, dangers that rarely, if ever, materialized. But things could happen and one should be paying attention, be ready, just in case. Money—or the lack thereof—haunted her imagination. When the bills arrived, she would arrange them according to due date in neat rows on the kitchen counter. Then she hummed and watered and worried and paced and rearranged things. She was way north of frugal. Scrooge was a spendthrift compared to Mother. She had lived through the Great Depression and by all accounts was still doing so—and thriving. The family income had never been above the official poverty line, but somehow his mother was able to squeeze the shit out of a buffalo nickel and had accumulated over fifty thousand dollars in savings by the time she retired.

A shiver of guilt, he shook his head and stared at the dancing red and green lights on his monitor, his mind flashed on the money he had lost in the market. More than she had saved. It took her a lifetime. He had lost it in less than two years.

He was bleeding money on the sharp edge of the learning curve. A good education was expensive. This time it would be different. He had learned his lesson. Things were turning around. Dark and unconvincing, his mantra of excuses hummed in tune with his mother's memory. It was just background static masking his panic as he fingered the ENTER button. The market was trending sideways within a fifty-point range. When it breaks out of this pattern to the upside he will buy. Or should he buy at the bottom of the pattern and pocket the extra fifty points? Why leave that fifty on the table? But what if it hits the lower boundary and keeps on going down? Again, he put his hands in his lap and watched. It was getting colder outside; the sleet was giving way to snow.

His "office" was little more than the spare bedroom with a large roll-top desk in the corner that held his computer. There were no pictures on the wall except the calendar pictures behind and to the left of the monitor. A bookcase stood against the wall to his right. One whole shelf was devoted to making money in stocks. A smooth, fake-leather three-ring binder leaned awkwardly near the far end of the shelf; a blunt reminder of where it all started.

Shortly after the death of his wife (breast cancer) and the check from the life insurance policy, a letter arrived inviting him to a free dinner where experts would offer guidance on wealth-making. Timing. His years as a teacher had provided financial security, but he never accumulated enough to be concerned about investments. But the life insurance money made everything different. With the downturn in the economy, and the Feds lowering interest rates, he could only get about two-percent interest in a traditional savings account. That was not good. He knew he needed to do more, but he didn't know where to start. Financial planner? Who could you trust? Mutual funds were not highly recommended, either. He was a loner and had always taken life in his own hands, made his own decisions, charted his own course. He had made mistakes, but had had some outstanding successes, too. But either way, he was fiercely proud of his independence. His mother was proud of him, too.

He had gone to the dinner. He signed up for a weekend study course, or was it a week long? He couldn't remember, nor could he recall the name of the person offering the course, but he *did* recall that it rhymed with "crook."

They studied charts on the fluctuations of a stock just before and immediately after a company split its shares. They studied the charts of IPOs. They talked about short-selling and futures and Calls and Puts. They studied formations in the charts that would indicate a bottom or a top, formations that would signal the best time to buy or sell. But one thing the instructors failed to mention was that "Way Crooked" (whatever his real name was, it sounded a lot like that) had lost over three hundred thousand dollars so far that year using the techniques that were being taught in the workshop. Techniques that were supposed to make one wealthy, extremely wealthy. Nor did they mention that Mr. Crook was being investigated by the Securities and Exchange Commission for false and misleading claims. It was over fifty thousand dollars later that he discovered the dark secrets of the glowing overstatements that filled his imagination with money and power and did serious damage to his trading account at the same time.

He had never mentioned any of this to his mother. He never would. The wind had gotten stronger and the humming in the fir tree was getting louder. Small snowdrifts were creeping across the lawn.

There! That was it. The candles on his chart had just completed a "W" bottom formation. *Click*. Seconds later a black window appeared on the monitor. The order was filled. The palms of his hands were sweating. He rubbed them on his jeans and then filled out a sell order and poised the cursor arrow on the SEND button and watched. The moaning in the fir tree was louder and dead leaves chased the snow in aimless circles and then scattered like startled birds as the wind shifted directions.

"Shit! It's going down. That's not supposed to happen. Go Up! Go friggin' up not down!" The voice startled him. He yelled again. It still didn't sound like his voice; it was more strained and angry than he remembered it sounding. Then his fist slammed hard on the desk. He grabbed the mouse and squeezed as if he could force his rage through the computer to Wall Street.

Click.

Who decided when a stock went up or down? Was it electronic

or was someone in a dark cellar making it all up? Supply and demand? He wasn't convinced. In his mind's eye he could see a frail, bony figure bent over a computer hissing in his Darth Vader voice, "This will show 'em," as he arbitrarily changed the prices— now up, now down—no rhyme or reason other than to devise evil ways to catch investors off guard and reach deep into their pockets. He felt violated and victimized by someone he would never meet, someone who existed only in his imagination. He had no tolerance for losses. Get out as quickly as possible. The black window confirmed the bad news. He'd lost ninety-seven dollars and the broker's fee. He hated losing. Outside, the humming stopped as if the wind needed to take a long deep breath before blasting the snow and leaves into another frenzy of confusion.

He was twelve years old again and Mother was humming and tapping a pencil on the ledger book. She was five cents off. Where had she spent that nickel? She emptied her purse for the third time and turned it upside down and shook it. No nickel. She stuck her hands deep into her pockets and then she checked the pockets of the coat she had been wearing. No nickel! He couldn't stand seeing her like this. He had to confess. He placed the chewing gum on the ledger without raising his head, without looking her in the eye. The whole lecture came pouring over him like hot wax. Money doesn't grow on trees and doesn't he know how hard Mother has to work to earn a nickel and how he will never have anything of value if he squanders all his money on chewing gum that will just end up in the waste basket anyhow and why doesn't he understand this and how stupid can he be? The words didn't stop until he cried long sobs and promised to never take a nickel again and assured Mother how much he appreciated her taking care of him. As he walked, still sobbing, to his room and closed the door, the sound of his mother's humming began to rise and fall with the rhythm of gum chewing

A buy order was open in the upper left corner of the monitor. The cursor arrow was on target. He didn't remember filling out the order, but there it was, buy at market price, just a click of the mouse away. The wind was picking up again and a few dead leaves tapped nervously on his window and the fir tree hummed.

About the author:

Terry Dickinson was born in 1942 in Greenville, Michigan, the middle son of a Protestant minister. He spent most of his growing years in or around Grand Traverse County. In 1965 he graduated from Central Michigan University with a degree in Mathematics and Physics. After teaching high school for ten years he made a career change into the field of art. Dickinson began his art career in 1974 in a big way, creating twenty-five feet by one hundred feet mural commemorating our nation's bicentennial. He continues painting murals as well as studio work today. As a preacher's son, Terry was immersed in words as he observed his father prepare for and present three sermons each week. As a teen he began keeping a journal, a habit that continued throughout his life. However, it wasn't until 2008 that Dickinson decided to submit any of his writings for critical examination. His first submission was a finalist in the Scribes Valley short story competition.

www.ingramcontent.com/pod-product-compliance
Lightning Source LLC
Chambersburg PA
CBHW051246170626
46809CB00004B/1519